Love Is…?

by

Barbara Donlon Bradley

Published by
Mélange Books, LLC
White Bear Lake, MN 55110
www.melange-books.com

ISBN:978-1-61235-125-4 Print

Cover Artist: Mae Powers

Love Is...?
Barbara Donlon Bradley

Love is many things, humorous, romantic, magical. In this variety of tales, Barbara Bradley will take you on a journey from the whimsical to the fantastic and pleasurable side of love.

A Wizard For Hire

Stephanie? A legend? Wizards? For real? When she flees down a corridor and finds herself in another world, Stephanie finds all her beliefs in question.

Crystals & Disappearing Cats, Barbara Donlon Bradley

Glenda's name has plagued her forever. Then she inherits a crystal that takes her to another world where witches are real, and she's mistaken for one.

Picture Perfect

Susan's homework assignment was simple. Bring something inanimate to life. Poor Warren. He didn't plan on being captured inside the manikin Susan decided to use.

A Fish Out of Water

Sarah McIntyre's klutziness could get her fired. Her last chance is a dinner function. Did fate or bad luck bring the stranger to her?

A Wizard For Hire

Chapter One

"Stop glancing at your watch," Stephanie said. "It isn't going to make this graduation move any faster."

Mia jerked her arm behind her and gave her boss a forced smile. "You know how much I hate these things."

Stephanie patted her on the back. She found attending the graduations of her "students" had started to bore her too, but she did this for the client. "Let them have their night, Mia. It's only a few hours."

"So who do you think will be the first one to leave?" Mia snagged a glass of champagne from a waiter's tray.

"I'd bet money on Bill and his wife. They're normally the first to arrive and to leave." Stephanie Powers, CEO of Power Imaging, gave her assistant a smile. "Then you can be second."

"Boss, if it weren't for your presence, I bet most would have high-tailed it out of here a while ago."

Stephanie elbowed Mia as one of their clients approached them. Time to focus. The man coming toward her made her skin crawl, but she smiled and showed her best business face.

"Miss Powers, thank you so much for inviting us here tonight."

"Mr. Tryst. I'm glad you were able to make it." He looked the part she created for him, wearing the classic designer suit she had recommended. His hair, cut short and feathered back, looked much better than the greasy ponytail he sported when he approached her to make him over. Yet he still looked, well, slimy.

"I would like you to meet my associate, Mr. Jolly. He's also interested in hiring you."

Stephanie wanted to scream and run the other way. She didn't want to go through the process again with another creepy man. Especially if he was friends with the first one.

"Call the office in the morning, and we'll see what we can do." She kept her smile pasted on and excused herself.

Mia was hot on her heels. "Are you crazy?" she whispered. "Mr. Tryst nearly cost us the entire staff."

"I couldn't be rude." Stephanie gave her assistant a sidelong glance. "But you could make sure we're booked for months."

"You hoping he will get tired of waiting and go somewhere else?"

"Yes."

"And if he doesn't?"

"We'll deal with that tomorrow. Tonight, we smile, tell our graduates they look great, and enjoy the party as best we can." Stephanie excused herself from Mia. She needed a little time alone.

One of the secluded love seats caught her eye. Far enough away from the rest of her clients, it would give her time to regain the composure she came close to losing a few moments ago.

"Are you sure this will work?"

Stephanie barely heard the voices. Her mind focused on the calming techniques she used, but the voices continued to intrude. She hoped they moved out of earshot quickly so she could try to relax.

"Yes. Miss Powers recreated me, didn't she?"

She frowned. Drat it, they weren't leaving, and they were talking about her.

"You do look like a proper businessman."

Stephanie felt a cold finger of dread snake its way up her spine as she recognized the voices.

"Yet you and I know the truth, eh?"

The other man laughed.

She started to get up, knowing she shouldn't eavesdrop on someone's private conversation. Before she could move, the two men moved closer, making it impossible for her to leave without being seen.

"Once we create the illusion of the men we are replacing no one will be wiser. We will infiltrate the right companies and gain what we need."

"There is a danger."

2

"My brother, there is always a danger when dealing with weapons of mass destruction."

"He will pay us well if we can complete our mission."

"And we will gain the respect we deserve."

What had she stumbled onto? Weapons of mass destruction? Who were these guys?

"Mr. Tryst?"

Oh dear. Mia had to be looking for her.

"Yes."

"Have you seen Miss Powers? I saw her heading this way a few moments ago."

Damn Mia for being so observant. If they knew she had overheard their conversation she might be in trouble.

"Oh, never mind. I see her."

Stephanie closed her eyes and prayed Mia had mistaken her for someone else. A few seconds later, her assistant smiled down at her. "I know you need a little time to yourself, but Mr. Carbuncle has been looking for you. He's getting ready to leave and wants to thank you for all you've done."

"Of course." Careful not to look at Mr. Tryst and his associate, Stephanie stood up, adjusted her skirt, and fell into step with Mia. The moment they were out of earshot, Stephanie started talking quickly. "While I am speaking to Mr. Carbuncle, I need you to get my car ready."

"What's wrong?"

"I overheard something I shouldn't have, and I'm afraid the people who were talking know it and aren't very happy." Mia started to turn her head. Stephanie grabbed her arm, hard. "Do not look.

"I believe we just helped out an international criminal," Stephanie continued. "And I want to put as much space as I can between me and them."

"What about the police?"

"I can't accuse them of anything. I only overheard bits and pieces."

Mr. Carbuncle smiled when he spotted her. Stepping close, he took her hand in his and brushed it with a light kiss then thanked her for all her help.

She nodded and hoped she gave the impression nothing was wrong, her mind preoccupied with how she would get out of there without making a scene.

After the longest two minutes of her life, Stephanie made the proper excuses and headed for the doors. Looking outside, she didn't see her car at the curb yet, but she hadn't seen Mr. Tryst or Mr. Jolly. If she were lucky, she'd still get away without being seen.

"Miss Powers. It is such a shame."

Stephanie didn't turn around. She knew the voice that made her skin crawl. Looked like her luck just ran out. Without thinking, she took off in a run. Her sensible heels didn't seem so sensible as she hurried down a flight of stairs.

She heard their shouts behind her, but didn't stop. Maybe her mad dash would alert people that something was wrong, and someone would come to her rescue.

She turned a corner and continued to run. Her feet screamed in protest, so as she hopped around another corner, she kicked off her shoes. The very smart business suit she always wore to these graduations hampered her movements. She flung her jacket behind her.

Stephanie spotted a secluded corridor to her right. If she could race down it fast enough, maybe her pursuers would think she went a different way and leave.

Pumping her arms and legs as fast as she could, she sped toward the hallway. Keeping up her dizzying pace as long as she could, she flew down the corridor as fast as her feet would take her. After a while, she had to stop. Her lungs burned from exhaustion.

Hands on her knees, she inhaled deeply. Marathon runner she wasn't.

The soft thud of a shoe vibrated through the corridor.

Stephanie glanced behind her in fear before looking at her stocking feet. They were still pursuing her. Sliding her hand through her hair, she started walking, her pace brisk. As long as she didn't see anyone behind her, she would keep the pace where she could handle it.

The lighting in this corridor was spaced further apart and dimmer than the other hallways, making visibility harder. That made her think about creepy crawlies. She hated them. Creepy crawlies always made her act like a fool. Stephanie couldn't keep from tiptoeing along the corridor.

"I am such an idiot," she muttered under her breath. Moving forward became mechanical. She wanted to stop and rest, but couldn't risk being caught. Every so often, she heard a faint sound. It was just enough to keep her going.

She walked for a long time, wondering where she'd be when she reached the end. Could this corridor be from another building? Or part of an underground system that connected several buildings together?

The corridor started to get brighter again. Stephanie felt herself relax. She must have reached the end. Now she could blend in with the crowd and make her way back.

Since she had traveled for a while, she knew she must be pretty far from the hotel. At least a couple of blocks. She didn't look forward to walking anywhere in her stocking feet.

Vines started to creep along the walls and ceiling, masking the concrete. Odd. Perhaps someone wanted to disguise the opening at this end and placed ivy all around it to conceal it. She'd bet it look like some sort of alcove from the outside.

The concrete floor gave way to sand. Wow, they did go all out. Walking in the sand made her tired muscles scream in protest. Getting the sand caught in her hose didn't help either. The intensity of the bright light ahead made her shield her eyes. The sun shouldn't be that bright now. Hadn't it set just as their party started?

Stephanie frowned. This wasn't right.

She ducked under some low hanging branches and gasped. She stepped out of the corridor and into a new world.

Chapter Two

"Wow." Stephanie stopped in her tracks.

Color exploded all around her. Reds, blues, greens, violets, every color she could think of blended with the foliage that surrounded her. Whoever had decorated this end of the corridor did a wonderful job. She felt like she was in a forest.

A noise close by reminded her she had been followed. Stephanie ran down a narrow path and ducked behind a small cluster of trees.

Mr. Tryst ran out into the light and stopped dead. Mr. Jolly wasn't as quick to stop. Both went down in a heap.

"Get off me, you imbecile." Mr. Tryst stood and dusted off his thousand-dollar suit. "We must find her, or she'll ruin everything."

"She couldn't have gone far." Mr. Jolly pointed to his left. "How about we split up? I'll go left, and you go right? This strange little garden must end somewhere."

Stephanie knew her hiding place wouldn't shield her from them for long if they started wandering around. She glanced at the corridor entrance, which now looked like a cave.

A cave? She shook her head. She didn't have time for this right now.

"Fine," said Mr. Tryst. "Except we can't leave this opening unattended, or she'll slip back through and call the cops."

Stephanie felt something push at the small of her back. Probably a wayward branch. She kept her eyes on Tryst and Jolly while she reached behind her, shoving away whatever it was. That didn't seem to work because it hit her a little harder.

She spun, expecting to find a small tree giving her a hard time. What she found took her breath away. A perfectly sculpted man stood in front of her wielding a small branch. A body so perfect, he reminded her of a marble statue.

A statue that moved.

The man she had mistaken for a statue stood a good head taller than her, well muscled, well, everywhere. Tight britches hugged his hips. A soft white linen shirt covered his chest. Okay, so it was opened to the waist, leaving a lot of glorious chest out there for her to ogle. Her heart started to beat a little faster.

Now if he would just get rid of the stupid stick with which he kept poking her.

"Do you mind?" she asked as she pushed the stick away again.

"Is that you, Miss Powers?" asked Mr. Tryst.

Why did she speak out loud? She knew better than that. It figured she'd let a silent hunk make her forget the situation. Ignoring her hunk, she turned back to see where Mr. Tryst was.

He still stood at the mouth of the cave, but now he had his gun out and waved it in her direction.

"I know you're out there, Miss Powers. Show yourself while you still can."

She wasn't that crazy. He'd fill her full of holes the moment he spotted her. Nope. She was going to stay behind the tree where she felt safe. Since her statue hadn't given her away yet, she hoped he would continue with his silence. If only he would stop jabbing her with that stick.

She felt the pressure against her back once again. This time she grabbed the stick and yanked. Stephanie thrust the same weapon at her statue.

"Stop jabbing me." She poked him. "With this stupid stick." She poked him again.

A bullet ricocheted off the tree behind her. In her anger, she gave herself away for the second time. A second report of the gun threw her into motion. She tackled her statue so a stray bullet wouldn't hit him.

They fell to the ground with a thud.

When she knocked into him, she thought of a brick wall. A warm brick wall with padding in all the right places.

She wanted to kick herself. She had to focus on surviving this, not thinking about a handsome man lying beneath her.

What kind of bizarre costume party had she walked into anyway? And why did she have to meet the only man around who didn't have the sense to go get the police when Tryst started shooting?

"That man out there is dangerous," she whispered. "We have to leave." She tried to clamber off him, but he held her fast. "Let go."

He tightened his arms around her and pulled her head against his chest. She struggled. Lying on this man's chest wasn't a good idea. She was already starting to have fanciful thoughts about him. This would just make it worse.

A soft murmuring came from his lips. Against her better judgment, it lulled her to rest against him, wrapping her in a cocoon of safety.

"I know you're there, Miss Powers." Mr. Tryst sounded very close, but all Stephanie noticed was her statue's warm chest. She could lie there all day and bask in that warmth.

A pair of Armani loafers came into view. Mr. Tryst was right in front of her. She stiffened and tried to lift herself up.

Steel arms tightened around her, holding her still.

"I know you are around here somewhere, my dear. You can't hide forever."

She stared at the chest. How was he shielding them from Tryst's view? It was impossible. Wasn't it? Yet Tryst couldn't see them, and he stood only inches away.

What was going on?

She heard shouts and felt pounding feet vibrate through the ground.

Men dressed like her statue slipped around them, surrounding Tryst. They gestured and pointed, speaking a gibberish she didn't understand.

Had she stumbled into some strange play? No. Tryst wouldn't go along with this. But how could this be real? Had she hit her head, and this was all a dream? She didn't remember falling or being hit in the back of her head, plus her imagination wasn't this creative so what was going on?

The men surrounded Mr. Tryst, touching his clothing and pointing to his shoes. Like flies, they swarmed around him and started to propel him away from where Stephanie lay.

Tryst tried to pull away from them, but they just laughed and continued to herd him away. "This isn't over, Miss Powers. My partner is still around here. You won't be safe for long."

Wherever here was, but she knew Tryst was right. She had to get to the police as soon as she could then go into hiding for a while. Maybe a long while if she was really smart.

Her statue relaxed his hold on her once they were alone.

"Thank you for protecting me." She stood up as quickly as she could. The less physical contact the better.

Minus her jacket, her silk shell left very little protection. She wrapped her bare arms around her middle. "Well, I must be going."

She found her arm trapped in a vise like grip. He started to pull her with him.

"No. I can't go with you." She tried to pull her arm free. "I have to go back home." And get back to reality.

He shook his head as he dragged her behind him. If she didn't know better, she'd swear he understood her.

"Look, you've been really nice and all." Although a bit silent. "But I need to go back to the cave."

Nothing.

She felt the first frissons of fear when the cave was no longer visible. How would she find her way back?

She started talking to herself. "Don't even know why I try. You probably can't understand a thing I'm saying anyway. But I sure wish you did. Then maybe I could make you realize how dangerous those men are and why I have to go back."

They wove through a small forest, one that wasn't like any of the ones back home. It was more like a hiking trail at a local park. No undergrowth, in fact there weren't even any leaves on the ground.

"I've never seen anything so clean," she murmured as she continued to look around. Her awe wiped away her fear for a moment. Her comment won her a strange look from the statue. "It would be nice if you talked because I feel like I'm losing my mind. I take a turn in a hotel corridor and find this place. I have no clue where I am, how to get back, or if I'm going crazy."

She stopped talking when the forest gave way to a beautiful meadow. Stephanie had to stop and stare at the splendor around her.

Flowers grew all over. Bright pinks, deep purples, powerful reds. The grass and leaves were an emerald color.

A gentle tug on her arm got her moving, but it didn't stop her from looking around and stumbling every once in a while because she wasn't watching where she was going.

They crested a hill and paused a few moments. Down in the little valley stood a small dwelling. There couldn't be more than two rooms in the whole building. It looked like something out of a *Grimm's Fairy Tale*. White washed walls, white picket fence, thatched roof. She stared at it in disbelief.

Another tug had her following him down the hill. She should be getting back to the cave, yet she trailed behind him until they reached the front door.

"You live here?" Her statue gestured for her to step inside. "Look. I don't want to intrude. Just take me back, and I'll be on my way."

He grabbed her wrist and started to pull.

She tried fighting him, but his strength overpowered her. He dragged her into the house, gave her a hateful glare, then went back outside, pulling the heavy wooden door shut behind him. Stephanie wanted to scream. She bet this guy was some kind of a masher, and now she was his prisoner.

Her first thought was to start screaming and banging against the door, but she realized that could bring her fate upon her a lot faster than her statue might be planning. Maybe if he took long enough, she could figure out how to get away. The windows looked easy enough to get through, but it was her statue that she had to be sure was out of the way. Peeking out the window, she spied the one thing between her and freedom. Her statue stood just outside. She also spotted a large group of people coming toward the small hut at a quick pace.

"Hey," she shouted.

Her statue turned toward the window. "You don't want them to know you are here."

Stephanie swore her jaw hit the ground. "You do speak."

"Quite well, although not half as much as you do. Now you must be quiet if you want me to protect you."

"Protect me? But—"

"If you don't be quiet, I will come in there and bind your mouth so you can't speak." He turned and faced the crowd.

Stephanie peeked out the window. They sure didn't look friendly. Over a dozen men surrounded her talking statue, and each of them held some sort of weapon. They murmured amongst themselves, waving little bags of leather and burning some foul smelling incense. They acted like they were afraid of him. Different people would back up when he turned his attention on them.

"Why have you come?"

"Wizard, we need your help."

Wizard? Had she been kidnapped by a Merlin wannabe? And why could she suddenly understand what they were saying?

Chapter Three

"No." He turned toward his hut and frowned when he spotted her at the window.

Stephanie backed up out of sight but continued to peer out the window.

"Please." The only woman in the crowd implored. Up until this point, she had remained hidden behind the shield of men. "My daughter."

Stephanie's statue turned and faced the woman. "Aren't you the woman who spits on the ground every time I pass by you?"

The woman hung her head.

"Why should I help you? You curse me each time."

"My daughter is innocent of my transgressions. Would you hold my sins against her?"

"Yes." He turned away.

"Please, she has had only eight seasons." The woman looked up at him. "She is all I have."

"If I help your daughter, will you still fear me?"

"Yes." She hung her head again.

Her voice was so soft Stephanie had to strain to hear her.

"Why?"

Stephanie wondered the same question. Why were they so afraid of him?

"Because of the legend."

Stephanie's brow crinkled. What legend?

"No."

"Please." The woman fell at his feet, her long brown braid brushed against his toes. "I promise not to interfere with the legend."

"You couldn't interfere with the legend if you wanted to." He stepped around her.

"What must I do to get your help?" asked the woman.

He stopped moving.

Stephanie saw his face from her vantage point. He closed his eyes and pinched the bridge of his nose. "You have nothing I want."

"Please. I can make you clothing, a rug to warm your feet. I am the best seamstress."

He paused for a moment. As he looked into Stephanie's eyes, he said, "A gown for my destined bride."

The woman looked up at him, her face pale. "Yes, my lord."

"About two hand spans will work. And I need it immediately."

The woman blanched at his words. "Yes, my lord."

He started toward the house.

"My lord? What about my daughter?"

"Make her bathe in the river five times." He looked at the woman. "Use root soap, nothing else. Once she has done that, send her to me."

"Yes, my lord."

"With the dress."

"Yes, my lord."

He walked to his front door, opened it, and turned. "Why are all of you still here? Needed to get a little longer look at your wizard?"

"No," stammered one man. "We found a stranger."

"Your priests found him."

The man nodded.

Stephanie wanted to laugh. Oh, he had them fooled. They thought him some great wizard because he knew a little about herbs and probably could tell them about things they didn't expect him to know, like the presence of Mr. Tryst.

"He claims there is a woman in our forest. A dangerous one."

She sighed silently. Mr. Tryst has been busy.

"There is no dangerous woman in this forest. Perhaps he misspoke. If he gives you more information then maybe I can find the woman for him." He paused for a moment. "But he does have a companion wandering in our forest. You might want to tell your guest his friend will come to harm if he remains in the forest too long."

Good one. Tryst might even wonder about the wizard because of this knowledge.

The small group started to wander back toward their town. Stephanie braced for her statue's entrance into the house. He sure wasn't friendly to the people he probably grew up with. How was he going to treat her?

The door banged open. His fierce scowl had her retreating behind a small table.

"I told you to stay out of sight."

"No one saw me." She didn't care how big he was. No one could talk to her like she was some sort of child and get away with it.

"They could have." He stomped up to the table. "And they probably would have turned you over to your friend if they had."

"He isn't my friend."

"I gathered that from his threats earlier. Yet you stuck your nose where it didn't belong."

"Excuse me?" She jammed her hands on her hips. "I wanted to go home. You are the one who made me come here instead of going back in the cave."

"You wouldn't have made it. His partner was just outside the cave waiting for you. In fact he is still there."

"And how would you know?" She crossed her arms over her chest. What a Neanderthal.

"You heard what they called me."

"Yeah, a wizard. I like how you got them fooled too. All you had to do is say just the right thing, and they fell over themselves trying to please you."

"Fooled?" The odd look on his face stopped her for a moment. He didn't actually believe he was a wizard, did he?

"So what is wrong with the girl?"

"Her eyes weep." He crossed to a large bookcase teaming with odd little trinkets.

"Crying isn't an illness."

"Not tears." Rummaging around, he pulled out a small bowl and a

14

leather pouch.

"Oh." The girl probably had pink eye. So why did she need to bathe?

"So she won't kill me with her stench when she comes for her medicine." He snagged a small gourd and placed all the items on a small wooden table.

Stephanie blinked. If she didn't know better, she'd swear he could read her mind.

"The villagers believe too many baths washes away their protection from illness." He started mixing the contents of the pouch with the liquid in the gourd.

Stephanie made a face. Just like the dark ages. "So you think she will bathe as you directed?"

"Yes. Her mother fears me too much not to do as I say." He crossed back to the bookcase and rummaged some more.

"Yeah, I heard that too. Something about a legend. What do they think you'll do, eat her daughter?"

"Something like that."

Stephanie frowned at the odd look he gave her. "So what is the legend?"

"It's no secret." He placed his hands on his hips when he didn't find what he was looking for.

"Well, I'm not from around here, so why don't you enlighten me."

"I have to go and get dinner. Make yourself comfortable." Before she could stop him, he walked back out the door.

He sure evaded that subject. She wondered why. Where was he going anyway? *McDonald's*?

Where exactly was she? Nothing made sense. She expected to come out of an alley a couple blocks away from the hotel, not, not here. Wherever here was.

So what was she going to do? Stephanie didn't know the way back to the cave, and according to her statue, Jolly lurked around it to stop her from returning to her world.

She knew getting hysterical wouldn't do any good. She had to keep her head. Think about something else.

Anything else.

She looked around the small home. The simple bookcase against the wall was crammed full of books, others were stuck in every spare nook and corner of the house. The furniture had to be handmade, lovingly sanded and polished to a beautiful sheen. The kitchen table folded so it could rest against the wall, the two chairs with it folded up and slid neatly into a small niche in the wall.

Stephanie stared at the door. Should she try to go home anyway? She hadn't seen him lock it. In fact, there didn't seem to be a way to secure the door. After a long debate with herself, she headed toward the door. Why did she hesitate? She needed to get back home. Jolly's presence shouldn't effect her decision.

Her hand closed around the handle of the door, and she crumpled to her knees. All her energy just drained right out of her. Dragging herself over to the wall, she rested her head on her knees.

She had never felt this bad, and it came on her all of the sudden. Maybe if she lay down for a moment she'd feel better.

~ * ~

Torin glanced in the window of his home just as he rounded the corner to the front door. The chatty woman was curled up in a ball on the floor. Guilt flickered across his face for just a moment. He had to keep her safe, and the spell he set was about the only thing he could use and continue her false belief. He snorted.

He wished he wasn't a wizard. To be normal had been something his magic couldn't do. His father told him he had a greater calling. So far, his great calling had ostracized him from the people he grew up with and had him curing boils and sick cows.

Gripping the handle, he pulled the door open, breaking the spell, and bringing fresh air into the small building. His new guest started to stir the moment she inhaled the fresher air.

Her lids slid up for a moment, revealing gray eyes framed by a ring of blue. The color of the prophecy.

He found them beautiful. Her thick black lashes made her eyes look so mysterious; he wanted to know what dwelled behind them. The prophecy be damned.

He studied her prone form. Her skin looked like satin, and he knelt

16

by her side to touch the smooth skin. It felt softer than he expected, like flower petals.

Her eyes opened again as he touched her face, never flinching as he gently slid his hand across her cheek.

"Are you okay?" He knew he needed to explain why he touched her if he wanted to keep her feeling safe.

"Yes."

"Let me help you up." He offered his hand, allowing her to make the first move.

She clasped his hand and pulled herself to her feet. "Not sure what happened. I just suddenly started to feel ill."

Torin knew she had tried to escape. The spell was designed to keep her from the door, but she must have pushed it hard for the spell to make her feel ill. Did she have powerful magic in her too? She didn't seem to believe in any power.

"Perhaps you should lie down for a while. There is a pallet up at the top of the stairs."

He watched those fascinating eyes widened. She didn't realize there was a second level to the house.

"No. I'm fine. Um, you were going out for food?"

He hadn't forgotten, but had left his kill by the front door when he had entered the house earlier. He had also picked up a few herbs he needed for the cure he started to work on.

"Yes. Are you hungry?"

"A little." A soft blush filled her cheeks. He found the color very becoming. Torin walked back to the door and brought in the small animal he had captured.

"Oh." She stared at the animal in horror. Poor rabbit.

He found her reaction odd as he placed the carcass on the small block in the back of his kitchen. With swift moments, he cut and skinned the animal then placed it in a pot on the stove. Taking vegetables out of a sack hanging on a peg, he cut them up then dropped them into the pot as well. Water was the last thing he added.

When he turned to face his guest, he found her face white. But before he could ask her anything, she started to babble. Again.

"How long have you lived here?" She turned away from the now bloodied block.

"Most of my adult life." He grabbed a bucket of water and rinsed the block off. The pink water dripped down onto the small rivets grooved into the floor.

"Why so far from the villagers?" She looked at his face and blushed again. "Oh. Never mind."

He watched as she moved about the room. Her grace made it look like a dance to his eyes. Torin would have to read the prophecy again to see how close she was to its fulfillment.

He hoped she was the one.

"So, um, what do you do out here?" She looked at him with wide innocent eyes.

She really had to talk all the time, didn't she?

"Live." He added several spices and thought for a moment before adding one more. Placing a lid on the pot, he murmured a few words to speed the cooking process and went back to the small bowl he had been working with earlier.

She nodded and clasped her hands behind her.

"Talking to you is like breathing to most, isn't it?" He stirred everything together and placed the bowl on a shelf.

"Of course not." She placed one hand on her hip and jutted it out saucily. The image made his pulse skip a beat.

"Then why must you strike up a conversation all the time?" He loved watching her. She filled the room with life. "Are you afraid of the silence?"

"No." She stopped for a moment. "Maybe."

"Why?"

"Where I live, silence can be scarier than the noise."

"What about the sound of the birds and the trees?" He needed to check the stew.

"It's more like car horns and people yelling."

"Doesn't sound like a very nice place." He pulled the lid off the top of the pot.

"I love the city, but you do have to get used to the hustle and bustle."

"I like to hear the sound of the birds in the morning." A deep whiff brought a smile to his face. He had added just the right amount of herbs.

She remained silent while he stirred the stew. He knew she did it to prove to him she could.

A hesitant knock on the front door startled them.

Torin crossed to the door first. Pulling it open, he faced a miniature version of the woman he had spoken to earlier. That didn't take long.

"Your mother has made the dress already?"

Silently, she held out a small bundle.

"Momma said she'll make two more. But she had almost finished this dress to see if someone would buy it. She knew it would fit." Her voice was so soft he had to strain to hear her. "She said you could cure me?"

"Come in."

Stephanie stared at the girl just as hard as she stared at Stephanie.

"Torin, you have found your bride!" The girl lost all her shyness with those words.

"What is she talking about?" A frown crinkled her brow.

"Why the legend, of course."

Chapter Four

"The legend?" Stephanie placed her hands on her hips again. The one thing her statue never explained to her. Perhaps the young girl in front of her might give her the information he didn't.

"Yesss." The little girl gave her a sweet smile, minus two front teeth. "You know the legend, don't you?"

"No."

"Oh." The little girl stared at her in awe. "That'sss part of the prophesssy. Torin. It hasss ssstarted, hasssn't it?"

"What has started?" Somebody had better start explaining something soon.

The little girl ran to Torin's overflowing bookcase, pulled a slender volume from one of the shelves, and walked back to Stephanie. The lavender cover was bound to the crinkled pages by twine.

She handed the book to Stephanie.

Frowning, Stephanie took the book and carefully flipped it open. Beautifully ornate lettering graced the first page. She stared at the page and realized she couldn't read the words. "What language is this?"

"The tongue of our ancccesssstorsss," lisped the young girl.

Stephanie handed the book back. "I'm sorry. I can't read this."

The young girl looked at Torin. "Ssshe doesssn't know our wordsss?"

"Don't tell me, that's part of the legend too." Stephanie wanted to roll her eyes. Just how gullible did they think she was?

The little girl nodded vigorously.

Torin took the book without comment. He stepped up to the bookcase and slid it back in its place before turning back toward Stephanie. "It's really nothing."

"I'd like to be the judge of that." Her curiosity got the best of her.

"Fine." He closed his eyes, focusing on something in his mind.

"Of fair hair and mind she shall come
beauty and poise are hers
new to our world
she won't understand our ways
what holds great meaning to us
will confuse her
but she will bring light to our world
she will help defeat the evil that will invade
through the darkness she will see the truth
that truth will pierce the heart of evil
removing it from our world forever
the Wizard will guide her
they will forge a bond that will change their lives
a bond that lasts forever."

Stephanie wanted to laugh. That sounded like one of those horoscope blurbs. Just vague enough for people to read whatever they wanted into it.

"See?" the little girl said to Torin. "She won't understand our ways."

"Umm." Torin pulled a stool out into the middle of the floor. "You came here for a cure, didn't you, Wymarda?"

The little girl turned toward Torin and nodded.

"Come and sit on the stool."

Stephanie watched the girl obey him. He grasped her head and tilted it up until he could look into her soft brown eyes. He grunted before moving to the shelf where he had placed the bowl earlier. He came back with it, dipped a finger into it, then placed the goo above, beneath, and on either side of both eyes. Tilting his head back, he murmured softly while he kept his fingers on her temple.

The air suddenly started to feel heavy in the room, as if some sort of energy was building. It felt like ants crawled on Stephanie's skin. Rubbing her arms, she glanced about, wondering where the weird sensation came from.

No one else seemed affected. Torin stood in front of the girl, head still tilted up, murmuring some chant. The young girl had her eyes closed, quietly sitting while she waited to be healed.

Pressure started to build in Stephanie's head. Pain sliced through her, making her rub her fingers against her forehead. Her knees gave way, yet she didn't fall. Some invisible force held her up, against her will, as the pressure grew. Suddenly, she felt a slight pop in her ears then the pressure disappeared. With perfect clarity, she knew the moment the young girl was cured. She could feel it in her bones.

~ * ~

Torin felt the power flow through her. She had the ability, just as he did, but didn't know it.

Focusing, he centered on the girl's eyes. His mind's eye flowed along her tear ducts. He found a small piece of dirt lodged within, creating the infection that caused her eye to seep constantly. He was amazed she didn't have more problems because of it. His magic floated the obstruction up to the top of the duct. The tears that he forced to flow washed it out.

He looked at Stephanie. He should have told her about the second verse of the legend, yet he couldn't speak the words earlier. Not until he was sure. Now he was. She was his destined bride. Something he knew she would fight when she learned the truth.

He stepped back from the young girl.

"Thanks to you, Torin." She bowed and smiled at him. "Today is a happy day."

"It is a good day."

The girl skipped toward the door, stopping just long enough to blow a kiss to Stephanie before she skipped out and down the path to the village.

"It won't be long now." Torin picked up the dress and handed it to Stephanie. "For you."

"Me?" Stephanie stared at the simple garment. The material looked soft, feminine, and not something she would normally wear.

"The rest of the villagers will be here soon. Your clothing marks you as an outsider. Dressing in the style of our people might help you blend a little better."

"They will say the same thing, won't they? That I'm some sort of prophecy fulfiller because of that legend."

He nodded.

"Then it won't make a difference what I wear."

"No." He put a lid on his jar of salve. Looking at her gray eyes had him wanting to do things to her he had no right to do, yet. "But how do you want them to perceive you?"

A quick nod of agreement from her answered his question. "Go up those stairs if you wish to have some privacy."

He finished cleaning up and checked on the stew again before she reappeared.

She was a vision. What a difference a simple dark blue dress could make on a woman. Where before she was all hard and sharp, now she was soft and flowing. It was also the first time he noticed the mark.

Right above her left collarbone rested a heart-shaped mole. Between her breasts hung an amulet of crystal. The ornate setting showed its age. Very old magic.

Unable to stop himself, he stepped up to her. With gentle fingers, he touched the crystal. Strong power pulsed within it. "It is beautiful."

"My great-grandmother's." Her breath caught in her throat when she felt his fingers touch the crystal. It hummed to life. Stephanie always feared when people handled it because it would judge the character of the holder. The stone remained clear when she could trust them, turned black when she couldn't. With Torin, a rainbow danced across the surface before it went clear again. That had never happened before. She knew she could trust him, but what did the rainbow mean?

He felt her heart start to beat rapidly when he rested his tanned hand against her fair skin. Was it fear or excitement that caused her reaction? The satin skin he wanted to explore so badly began to heat beneath his hand. Her chest started to rise and fall faster.

"And this?" he asked as he brushed his fingers against the heart shaped mole.

"Birthmark." Her voice sounded throaty, deeper, sexier and oh so arousing.

"Hmmm." Torin bent and placed a soft kiss against it. Her scent, soft, feminine, uniquely her, filled him. The pulse in her throat beckoned next. It fluttered erratically as he pressed his lips against it. A flick of his tongue brought a soft moan out of the delicious throat he made love to.

Without thought, he wrapped his arms around her, bringing her closer. Feeling the press of her body against him caused desire to race through him. He sucked air into his lungs to fight the burning need he felt.

Small sharp teeth nipped at his ear, drawing a groan from him. His lips searched for hers. They moved across her jaw and cheek to find the warm haven of her mouth.

What he found was heaven. He lost himself in the sensations. The taste of her, the brush of her tongue against his. He wanted more. He needed more. Torin's heart beat rapidly in his chest.

His lips traveled back down her neck to the top of the gown. The soft blue gown gathered in his hands and lifted easily. Underneath he found the oddest garments. Ones that made his blood boil. "You are beautiful."

His finger glided along her satin smooth skin. He eased the strap off one of her shoulders and kissed skin beneath. The salty sweet taste of his skin begged for more of his kisses.

A soft moan escaped her lips, spurring him on. Her soft flesh carried a unique scent. It filled him. Closing his eyes, he moved them to the loft where his pallet lay. He also took care of his clothing at the same time. Being a wizard had some good points.

Her hair spread on his pallet, burning an image into his mind that would last him a lifetime. Golden tresses he wanted to bury his face in. She opened for him, not hesitant in her sexuality.

His body tightened at the thought of their bodies surging together as one. The need to be inside her overwhelmed him. Pressing his body against hers nearly undid him. Nothing mattered except feeling her body wrapped around him.

He feared she wouldn't be ready for him, but when she wrapped her legs around him to urge him on, he surged into her. Joy embraced him. Her body fit him like a glove squeezing him to ecstasy.

"Please." She begged him to take her.

With quiet deliberation, he started to move inside her. Their breathing blended with the sounds of the forest. As he slid in and out, he felt her body tremor. His reacted in kind. She tightened against him, and he felt himself swell to increase the delicious friction. The better it felt, the faster he moved. He could feel the pinnacle approaching. He raced to the finish line, bringing Stephanie along with him. It started slowly, but he could feel his body start to splinter then he felt like he was soaring. Like he dove off the cliffs near his home, slicing through the air toward the water below.

Stephanie's body tightened like a bow. As her body reached her orgasm, he felt her squeeze him, milk him dry. When her body relaxed, he did too.

"Wow." It was the first word Stephanie had spoken in a while. Now he knew how to keep her quiet.

A bang at the door jolted them. He rested his head against hers as he wished the villagers would abide by his wishes and leave him alone.

"What?" She sounded breathless.

"Someone's here." After placing a quick kiss on her forehead, he dressed and went to the door. He took a deep breath to calm himself, placed his hands on the wooden panel and concentrated on what stood on the other side.

The entire village surrounded his home, including the stranger Stephanie was trying to avoid. The man had been carried to his cottage on a litter like some sort of king. Torin wondered what this man had told them to gain this kind of power. The sound of wood creaking had him turning back to look at her.

"Something wrong?" She had dressed and come down the small ladder to join him.

"Your friend is out there too." He stepped toward her.

"Who?" Stephanie moved toward the window. One glance had her skidding back to him. "What do we do now?"

"I can be my normal belligerent self and see if I can get them to leave."

"He won't take no for an answer, you know." She bit her bottom lip.

"We have to face him sooner or later anyway. We can go now, while he has the upper hand, or we could go later, at our own time."

"I won't let him control me."

"I agree." He smiled, brushed a stray hair from her face then planted a quick kiss on her lips. "Don't let them see you. If they start to come in the house, there is a secret room behind the bookcase. Move the table, and you'll see the opening." He squared his shoulders then headed to the door. A quick glance behind him made sure she was out of sight.

Another deep breath and he opened his door. "Why are you here?"

"We want the girl," said Tryst.

"Wymarda has already gone home." He started to close his door.

"I'm talking about Stephanie Powers."

Torin debated. He could just ignore this man, but he threatened Stephanie's safety. He stared the man down. "And who are you?"

"Your new God."

Torin laughed. "Have they told you what I am?"

"Some sort of magician."

"A wizard," someone near Tryst hissed. "He can get angry if you use the wrong title, and you don't want him angry."

"So, what is your name? Merlin?"

Torin crossed his arms over his chest. This little man had no clue with whom he dealt. Just like Stephanie, he didn't believe in the power. Perhaps a little show of what he could do would change the man's mind.

"Who is this Merlin?" Torin asked, arching one brow. "Some sort of mediocre magic man?"

"Just like you?"

The only sound heard was a collective sharp intake of breath. None of the villagers would look him in the eye.

"So you think I can't do any damage to you with my abilities?" Torin looked at the man propped up on pillows. In his mind, he imagined the man with a pillow stuffed in his mouth.

Tryst's face showed his shock when he suddenly couldn't breathe. He clutched at his throat, trying to loosen whatever blocked his breathing.

No, that wouldn't work. This Tryst would probably blame his constrictive clothing. Maybe he should give him a hot foot.

Tryst dragged in great gulps of air when he found he could breathe again. His face pinched up as he started to fan his foot.

Torin decided against that too. A hot foot could be explained. He had to make this man realize the depth of his powers.

"Tell me, what could I do to make you believe I am what they claim? Perhaps I should bind you?"

Tryst found his arms and legs locked together. "Hey!"

"Hmm, how about if you were to suddenly find yourself hanging upside down?"

The silly man yelped when he was indeed hanging upside down.

Torin smiled when the villagers started to move away from Tryst. "If you're a God, why aren't you stopping me?"

Tryst struggled for a small black cylinder, held it for just a few seconds before it fell to the ground several feet below his head. He tried to reach it, but Torin lifted him higher. He wouldn't let Tryst reach the weird object.

Torin called it to him. It slid along the ground before it floated above everyone's head and to his hand. "A weapon, I assume?"

"Give that back."

"Why?" Torin tucked the weapon in his waistband. "So you can try to hurt me? That wouldn't be very smart of me, would it?"

"Now." He spoke to the villagers. "Leave. I've met your God, and I'm not impressed." He released his hold on the man, allowing him to crash to the ground. Torin turned away from the crowd and started to enter his house once again.

"I want the girl."

"I know of no 'girl'. Now go away." Torin continued into his house.

"One of the villagers said you have her here."

He turned in anger. His eyes glowed angrily, wind whipped around, causing leaves to fly. Torin's hair danced around his face. "I said go! Do not fire my wrath any more. The woman you search for will come to you when the time comes."

He entered his cottage and the door closed behind him with a thud.

Stephanie stood in front of him.

"You *are* a wizard?"

Chapter Five

"I already told you that." He moved further into the room.

"True." She nodded. "But where I come from, no one has the powers you do. At least I've never seen anything like that before."

Her look of awe surprised him. Perhaps now she would listen. "You didn't stay hidden."

"I did, but I had to see what was happening." She looked up into his face. "So I peeked a little."

"You have never seen such before?" Should he tell her she had the same power? Would she believe him if he did?

Perhaps, if he asked just the right questions, she would realize the truth herself.

"Except for television."

"What is television?" He couldn't help asking that question. There was so much about her and her world he didn't know, and now he needed to know. The few forays into her world left him confused and curious.

"A type of entertainment."

Entertainment? Did she mean tricks? How could he convince her magic was real if she thought otherwise? He needed time to think about this. "Hungry?"

"Not really."

"Suit yourself." Torin walked to a small alcove, returning with cheese and bread. He set the light fare on the table before pulling out one of the chairs. "Confronting the village idiots always makes me hungry."

Stephanie watched him, but made no move toward the table. "Tryst was the real idiot. But he wouldn't have believed them either. Your type of power doesn't exist in my world."

"Are you sure?" He bit into the sharp tangy cheese.

"Believe me, if someone had that type of power, they would have tried to take over the world by now. Greed is a terrible thing, and it rules my planet."

"Why don't you do something about it?" He tore off a piece of bread and popped it in his mouth.

"There are people who do."

"I'm not talking about other people. I mean you." He rested his elbows on the table while he waited for her answer.

"What can I do?" She placed her hands on her hips.

"One grain of sand moves, and a foundation can crumble. One person can do a lot, but they must believe in themselves."

~ * ~

That was exactly what she told her clients when they first started orientation. When did she stop listening to her own words? When had she turned complacent?

Stephanie looked around the room again. She couldn't look into those knowing eyes. He was right. She complained about the way life was but never did anything to change it. The heady aroma of the stew floated around her head. Against her comment of not being hungry, her stomach growled angrily.

Torin just looked at her with a half smile.

"Okay. So maybe I'm a little hungry."

"Help yourself." He pointed to the platter filled with cheese.

"What about your stew?"

"That will be our dinner."

She nodded. Torin still sat in his chair, elbows propped up, his chin resting on his hands.

Stephanie hoped she wouldn't make a fool of herself when she wrestled the chair out of the slot. She gripped the chair and started pulling.

What was the chair made out of? Granite? It hadn't budged an inch.

The heat of his body brushed against hers when he reached around her and pulled the chair out with ease. "You are stubborn. If you had asked, I would have gotten it."

"Yeah? In my world, a gentleman would have gotten the chair before I would have had to ask."

"Is that why you tried to get it yourself?" Torin propped the chair against the table. "Because you don't believe I am a gentleman?"

"No. Well." How could she answer that question? "I thought I could do it myself."

"And you would have if you had bothered to look at the slot before pulling. You have to lift the chair before pulling it out. It sits in a small grove to keep it in place." He opened the chair then sat back down. "Tell me about Mr. Tryst."

"I don't know that much, unfortunately. He came to my firm wanting an image make over."

"Then why is he chasing you?"

"I overheard something I shouldn't have." She broke off a small piece of the cheese block in front of her. The fact the cheese was purple made her hesitate. She looked up and found Torin watching her. "He plans on hurting a lot of people in my world. I don't know how or why, but I know enough to be a threat to him."

"Then he must not go back to your world."

"And how can I stop him?" She popped the cheese into her mouth and bit. The creaminess and sharp tangy flavor surprised her.

Torin only smiled at her.

"Look, if you have stuff to do, go ahead and do it." Trying to convince him of the danger wouldn't be easy. It wasn't his world being threatened.

"Have you ever been to my world before?"

She shook her head then took another bite. This place shouldn't exist. How could she have been here before?

"Would you like to go for a walk? There is much I want to show you. I call them my little treasures." He stood and offered her his hand.

Perhaps a walk would allow her to clear her mind so she could think of a way to stop Tryst. Walking always helped her when she had to work out problems before.

Her chair scraped against the floor when she pushed it back.

His long callused fingers wrapped around hers as he led her out the door and around back of the small hut.

Stephanie heard the cries of birds, the soft tittering of small forest animals, the trill of crickets. She never realized how alive a forest was until then. Running water could be faintly heard between the sounds of the other animals. It grew louder as they walked.

"Are you thirsty?" Torin asked as he pushed a small curtain of vines to the side. He pointed to a small rock formation. Clear spring water pooled in a small bowl at the top of the formation, with a constant trickling over the edges.

"How beautiful." She looked around in awe. The only thing she could compare it to was a small grotto. The fountain sat on a stone floor, surrounded on three sides by a natural rock wall. Vines climbed the walls, while trees in the area gave a natural covering overhead.

"There's more." He gave her a secret smile, and after taking her hand, he led her out of the grotto and down a stone path.

Stephanie followed behind him feeling like a child in a candy store. She kept staring around at the raw wonder surrounding them.

"Watch your step," Torin said as he started down the side of the mountain.

"These are man made." Stephanie grabbed his hand harder. The stairs wound down below them, going on forever. Her fear of falling reared its ugly head when she looked down.

Her first instinct was to plaster herself against the nearest wall, but the stairs had no wall.

"This is part of the old fortress. Once the wars stopped, the villagers moved out to the fields to better tend their crops, and the fortress fell to disrepair."

She didn't respond. She couldn't.

"Stephanie?" Torin turned around to face her. He stopped moving the moment he saw her face. "Are you all right?"

She nodded without releasing her deathlike grip.

He touched her face. She could feel the tick in her jaw start to pulse. Pretty soon her eye would start twitching.

He scooped her up in his arms and continued down the stairs. Stephanie transferred her steel grip to his shirt, as if that would stop her from falling once she started.

"I never took you for a usan."

"What is a usan?"

"Someone who has fears like yours."

"Oh." She looked up into his rugged face. "Where I come from, we call them phobias."

"Ah, so it is common where you are from, too?"

"Mine isn't that bad. I just make sure I stay away from rickety stairs and ladders."

"So it isn't the height that bothers you?"

"No. It's the falling. I can ride roller coasters and travel at great speeds, but put me on a Ferris wheel, and I'll freak out."

"Freak out. That is an interesting phrase."

"It means get a little crazy. I must have something secure under my feet, or my fear of falling will take control."

"Yet, you are fine now."

Stephanie wanted to argue with him, but he was right. The moment he picked her up, she felt more secure. As they spoke, she'd forgotten her fear and relaxed her grip on his shirt.

He stopped moving and started to release her legs.

Stephanie wrapped them around his waist as she squeezed her eyes shut.

"Stephanie."

"Yes?"

"We're safe now."

She opened one eye and looked around. They were on solid ground once again. Stephanie could feel the heat from a deep red stain spread up her neck and cross her cheeks. She found herself nestled against Torin in a very provocative way. He seemed to enjoy it, too, if the solid length she felt pressing against her was any indication.

She unwrapped her legs and slid down his front. That didn't help matters at all. He watched her with darkened eyes. Her breath came a little shorter. Her libido definitely found him very attractive, and his playing hero increased it tenfold.

Clearing her throat, she hoped to break the sexual tension growing between them. Once again, she found her hand enveloped in his.

"You must be very quiet." He put his fingers to his lips as he snuck around a corner. Stephanie found herself tiptoeing behind him.

They stopped suddenly. Torin pulled her in front of him, wrapped his arms around her and whispered. "Watch."

He toed a small rock, gently kicking it into the center of another old section of the fortress. Stephanie thought it looked a bit like a bedroom. The walls were all yellow.

The small rock landed in the center of the room, causing a ripple effect. What she thought were yellow walls started to come alive. Thousands of wings took flight.

"Butterflies," she breathed in awe as the colorful winged creatures pushed off the surfaces they rested on and soared up over her head. The spot they stood in remained free of the butterflies, so they could watch the glorious sight without being in the way.

Stephanie didn't know how long they stood there watching. She didn't care. The beauty he'd shown her touched her deeply. It showed a romantic side she found very attractive. The feelings she was developing for Torin were growing too fast for her liking, yet she found she couldn't stop them. He was different.

She sighed when the butterflies had either flown away or settled back down. Before she could thank him, he tugged on her arm to lead her away. Goodness, what was he going to show her next?

He looked back at her with a grin to stop her heart.

"More?" she asked.

"Just one more place."

"The best for last?" What could possibly be better?

"Something like that."

"How do you plan on topping the butterflies? I've never seen anything like it." She watched her feet as they walked through another section of the old fortress. Here the stone floor was uneven. If she weren't careful, she'd do a nosedive onto it. She didn't want to make that kind of impression on him.

"I'm glad you liked it. I like to go there to think." He continued to guide her through the ruins. "We have a bit of a walk from here."

"So it's not part of the fortress?" She stepped out into the sunlight and had to shield her eyes.

"No." He headed for the forest nearby.

"So what is it?" He just gave her that heart-stopping smile again and picked up the pace. It didn't take her long to figure out he wasn't going to tell her anything. Asking questions was out, too. She was hurrying to keep up with him. His long strides outpaced hers two to three.

She followed the path to the right and had to stop short once again because Torin's immovable body suddenly stopped in front of her. Not being able to stop fast enough, she skidded into his back before she lost all her momentum.

"Close your eyes."

"What?" She looked up to find Torin smiling.

He placed his hands over her eyes before moving her around so she stood in front of him again.

The sound of his voice so soft next to her ear sent goose bumps down her spine. They moved as one down the path. A couple of turns and they stopped. "Okay. Now you can open them."

Stephanie opened her eyes and gasped.

Chapter Six

Torin's heart raced. Each place he took her brought her deeper into his world. She didn't know the significance behind the places they visited, but soon she would. He wondered how she would react when she learned the truth.

He could feel moisture start to bead on his skin. How he loved this place. His haven from the storm.

Her sharp intake of breath had him holding his. Her reaction would prove the legend true or false.

"Torin?" She gripped his arm tight. "Where are we? Paradise?"

He closed his eyes, afraid she'd see the joy that had leaped into them. Those were the exact words she had to use to fulfill the prophesy. Now all he had to do was show her the way.

"I like to think so."

He watched as she drank in the sight of the waterfall cascading down into the pool of water. He felt her inhale the fragrance of the wild flowers in bloom. Tears came to her eyes as she viewed the riot of colors from the flowers growing in odd nooks and crannies along the fall.

He released his breath. The view moved her as much at it moved him. Torin grinned as he stepped to the edge of the path t. With a wink, he dove into the pool several feet below them.

"Torin?" She gripped the edge of the rock formation near her.

"Come in, Stephanie." He hoped the height wouldn't scare her. She was only a few feet above the water.

"I can't."

"Can't you swim?" He hadn't thought to ask her that one.

"Of course. But what if someone comes along?"

His brow furrowed while he tried to figure out her question. "No one comes here but me. They're afraid of the magic."

"Oh." She glanced around.

Torin couldn't figure out what she was waiting for. Didn't she believe him?

"Turn around."

"Why?"

"So I can undress." A pretty blush filled her cheeks. "I don't want to ruin the dress."

He shrugged as he did as she asked. Women could be so strange at times. The dress could withstand the water.

Maybe clothing in her world couldn't. He was about to explain that to her when he heard a slight splash. Turning around, he found her in the water, moving like a water sprite.

"This is like bath water," she said as she swam up to him.

"Several hot springs feed into the creek that feeds the waterfall." He saw a bare shoulder peak up out of the water. His pulse started to race.

"This is wonderful." She dipped her head back.

Torin hoped to get a glimpse of something more than a shoulder then chastised himself. First things first.

"There's something I'd like to show you."

"No more." She pushed away from him. "I want to enjoy this some before we go off on another one of your quests."

"It's not a quest," he said, following after her. A small strap appeared on another bare shoulder. His heart beat hard when he realized she wore the strange undergarments.

"It can wait, right?"

"Yes." He was too busy remembering what the strap belonged to. He'd show her the ancient stone later.

Torin glided a little closer. "Your dress would have been fine in the water. I wash my clothes here all the time."

"Maybe, but it would have dragged me down too much, and I was afraid of getting it caught on something." She looked away from him.

"There's something you're not telling me." He sensed her hesitation but didn't understand it.

"The dress was made out of gauze."

Most of the women in the village wore gauze dresses. Wool was too heavy this time of year. "Yes?"

"Getting it wet would have made the material transparent." There was that pretty blush again.

"Just like it will when you don it later."

"I'll just dry off before I put it back on."

"So you will sit out on a rock naked while you wait for your skin to dry so you can put on a dress so no one can see what it hides? That makes no sense."

"I'm not naked, and yes it does make sense."

"You are not naked?" He touched the bare shoulder. "Then what is this?"

She looked up at him, her eyes wide. She pulled a strap like he saw on the other one up onto the top of her shoulder. "My underwear."

"Underwear." He could feel his body responding to just the thought of what she hid beneath. His fingers caressed the silken strap before sliding down over her shoulder. "So soft."

Her lips parted as she exhaled a pent up breath. Torin couldn't stop looking at those luscious lips, so full and inviting. He had to taste them.

~ * ~

Stephanie's insides melted when she felt his callused hand slide over her shoulder. No man's innocent touch had made her react like this before. Butterflies took flight in her stomach when she noticed his eyes darkening as they stared at her lips.

His lips gently touched hers, and molten heat started to run through her veins. Her body acted on its own, wrapping itself around his like a second skin. They were moving too fast, yet she couldn't stop when he deepened the kiss.

Her heart pounded in her ears, the butterflies danced in the core of her. Her fingers glided through his hair. The wet strands felt like silk. The roughness of his shirt made her realize he had too much on. Her fingers made short work of the tunic he wore. Leather ties came free and floated away on the water. The rest she pushed down his arms as far as she could.

A sigh escaped her when she felt his hot flesh against her own.

Stephanie didn't know what was happening to her. She had never felt so wanton before. Like a fever, desire had taken control. Kisses branded her neck. His large hands gently caressed her. Their clothing vanished under the magic of his need. Her body burned with a heat only Torin could put out.

She couldn't remember when they floated under the waterfall, or even left the water, but the moment he entered her, time stood still. Energy burst forth, enveloping them in its light. It flowed through her, filling her with a strength she had never felt before.

Did Torin feel it too?

Ancient words spilled from his lips, words she didn't understand, yet did. The language was beyond her, yet the meaning was still there. Tender, loving.

The heat continued to build in her, pushing her harder and faster. Then it happened. Her body shook from the power of the explosion. Her soul soared over the small lake and waterfall.

"Paradise," she whispered.

~ * ~

Torin had never felt such power before. It called to him, seducing him into a vortex of desire he had never felt before. He closed his eyes as he tried to calm his racing heart.

He had said the ancient words. Why, he wasn't sure. Something drove him to mutter them at the height of their lovemaking. Binding words that couldn't be undone once spoken.

Rolling over, he propped himself up on one elbow and studied her features. Such delicate beauty hid so much power. He wondered if she realized what happened between them while caught in the throws of passion. The exchange of power and their souls.

They could never be apart now. He hadn't planned on binding her to him in the way of the ancients, but it had been done. Now he would just have to explain.

He chuckled. If she behaved as she had since they had met, she would deny the bond. At least until the pain of separation became too much. Then she would probably get mad at him.

He looked up at the huge tablet that dominated the room. The legend would have to be the first thing he explained. One denial at a time.

~ * ~

Stephanie opened her eyes and found the ceiling of a cave above her. Tiny indentations etched the walls and ceiling. It took a few minutes for her to realize that ceiling wasn't covered with etchings, but shot through with gold. Some of the veins were as big as her fingers. The effect made the ceiling look like the stars and the moon.

38

Her body still felt boneless. She had been with her share of partners over the years, yet what she just experienced made her feel like a virgin all over again. Her heart still raced, and she could still feel little tremors shooting through her. "Talk about the earth moving."

She turned to where Torin lay, expecting to find him asleep. To her surprise, he lay on his side, gloriously naked, giving her that heart-stopping smile.

"That smile of yours is dangerous."

"It is?" He looked at her curiously. "Why is that?"

"It makes my heart do strange things."

His smile deepened. "Like what?"

Oh, no. Stephanie wasn't sure she could handle another earth shattering orgasm so soon. She needed to get the conversation onto neutral territory.

"Where are we?"

"This is my cave."

Figured. She looked around, rolling onto her stomach to be able to get a better view. That's when she remembered she was as naked as Torin.

He stood up and offered his hand.

"You are shy now?" He shook his head, still grinning. "Wait here."

A few moments later, he came back with a long cloth.

"Sometimes I rest here, so I always keep something to ward off a chill. Wrap yourself in the blanket."

"Thank you." Stephanie was touched that he thought of her sensibilities, as silly as they were. The cloth was so soft and supple she couldn't see why he called it a blanket.

Once the cloth had been anchored properly, she followed him deeper into the cave. In the center stood a massive obelisk. Stephanie had never seen anything like it, unless you counted *2001: A Space Odyssey*. It looked like black marble with ancient runes engraved on it.

"Interesting centerpiece."

"I know." He smiled again while handing her a bit of cheese and something to drink. "It's wine. Everything else seems to go bad here."

"Even water?" She took a sip.

"Turns brackish, can't explain it. I've tried all kinds of things, but nothing works."

"So what does it say?" She tugged the cloth a little tighter around her as she circled the stone.

"It holds the legend."

"Your legend?" She saw him nod out of the corner of her eye. The obelisk demanded most of her attention. "There seems to be a lot more here than the passage you quoted earlier."

"The villagers only know the first stanza, and they only found out about that accidentally."

"Not something you wanted them to know?"

"No." He sat down in front of the obelisk and patted the ground beside him. "You saw one mother's fear over what little she did know."

"Will you tell me the rest of the legend?" Stephanie sat beside him.

"If you are sure." He gazed up at the words. "Do you want me to start from the beginning?"

"Sure."

"Of fair hair and mind she shall come
Beauty and poise are hers
new to our world
she won't understand our ways
what holds great meaning to us
will confuse her
but she will bring light to our world
she will help defeat the evil that will invade
through the darkness she will see the truth
that truth will pierce the heart of evil
removing it from our world forever
the Wizard will guide her
they will forge a bond that will change their lives
a bond that lasts forever"

Stephanie waited when Torin paused. He acted like he didn't want to read the rest.

"Her hair, golden, her eyes, blue and gray,
this young woman will refuse the way
her life belongs elsewhere she'll cry
and in the beginning her help she'll deny
but jokester and teasers will abound

and refusing to give any ground
will force the damsel from another world
to make a choice and be heard
She will fight to save her love
the one man she will put above
her home, her life.

Fair of heart and of mind
but at first she will be blind
Darkness will surround the two
Prisms of color will light the way
right is wrong
wrong is right
red, yellow, blue and white
A twist of fate
the trust of love
one small sacrifice will gain it all
one false step will lose it
in the end the tryst will fall
and Stephanie will answer the call
of her true loves heart."

Stephanie's jaw dropped. The poem named her. "That can't be right."

"Read it yourself." Torin gestured toward the obelisk.

"I can't read this language."

"You haven't tried to read the stone." He took her hand and placed it on the black marble. "You will be able to make out some of the words because they are from your world."

Stephanie stood up. Like before there were a lot of words she didn't recognize, but as she studied the strange script she found more words did look familiar. They were close enough to English for her to figure out what they meant.

Her heart stopped when she read the last line.

Torin and Stephanie, 992 A.D.

Chapter Seven

She read their names. That couldn't be. Stephanie stood up. It would mean she was supposed to be here, to be Torin's mate. To give up everything she had accomplished so far in her life, her friends. Everything. "No."

"No, what?"

"I don't believe this. Somehow you rigged this whole thing."

"So you think I met you, raced down to this secret place of mine, carved the ancient runes into the stone, and then made sure the villagers knew about it so I could fool you?"

When he put it like that, it did sound a bit ridiculous. "You forgot that you had to hide the shavings from the stone, too."

He tried so hard to keep a straight face. "And had to come up with that rhyme."

"Yeah, about that. What the heck were they going for? The first section is completely different than the other two."

"I don't know. I studied it for several years." He walked around the obelisk. "I haven't figured it out."

"And how did the villagers know this was about you? No names were mentioned in the part they know."

"My mother." Torin walked away from Stephanie. "She found the ancient stone when I was still wee. The stone changed her. She used to give the villagers their herbs and medicines when they needed it, but never considered herself any more than a midwife. The moment she clapped eyes on that stone, she suddenly started to talk about prophecy. Several times, she would make a prediction and be right.

42

"After a while the villagers started to fear her. They didn't want to have anything to do with her, where before, although they would make fun of her talents, they would never shun her. She had helped just about everyone in the village."

"And that changed because of the stone?"

"Yes."

"Why? How did they know she told the truth?" It didn't make sense to Stephanie. Why would they put so much trust in this woman's words?

"Because she showed the stone to someone, and the moment he told everyone she spoke the truth, he collapsed and died. They all thought powerful magic had killed him. From that point on, she was the mother of the man in the legend."

Now Stephanie understood. They never feared his mother, but they had always feared Torin, and since he probably was with his mother every time she went into the village, he thought they were shunning her without realizing it was him they feared all along. The sadness around his eyes had her rethinking those thoughts. Maybe he did know after all.

"What do you mean by magic? I haven't seen anything I'd consider magical."

"What would you like to see?"

"I don't know." She averted her eyes as she racked her brain. What was it wizards were suppose to do? "How about a ball of light?"

"Any particular color?"

"Purple?"

He held out his right hand. Mumbling softly, he started to wave his left hand over the right.

Stephanie watched a flame leap into existence in his hand. As his right hand continued to move over the top of the left, the pyre of fire continued to grow in size, slowly rounding out like a small ball, and changing to lavender before deepening to a violet color.

"How did you do that?"

"Would you like to hold it?"

"Really?" She looked up at him, afraid to believe she could actually hold it in her hand. He stepped up to where she sat and held out the light.

She jumped to her feet, dusted her hands off, and held them out. "Now what?"

"Relax." He smiled at her. "Level your hand out. That's good."

Stephanie watched in awe as he gently placed the ball in her hand. She could feel the shots of electricity as she held it. The ball felt alive. She wrapped her hand around the ball, laughing when she could hide the light within her clasped palms.

"I have never seen anything like this," she said when she moved one hand, and the ball sprang back to the size it had been when Torin handed it to her. He took the ball back, and with a wink and a quick puff of breath, the ball disappeared.

"How did you do that?" Stephanie walked all the way around him, looking for wires or mirrors. Anything to prove it was all a trick, because if it weren't, she'd have to reevaluate her whole way of thinking.

"Magic."

"You mean illusions." She noticed the frown on his face. "Slight of hand, misdirecting my attention so I'm not seeing how you pulled it off."

"You still think it is fake?"

Stephanie stopped moving. The sadness in his voice made her feel like a heel. She suddenly frowned. Was he shrinking? She actually had to look down at him now to make eye contact.

After glancing down, she wished she hadn't. Her feet were about a foot off the ground. "Put me down."

"But it's just an illusion." Torin mimicked.

"Torin, if you know what is good for you, you'll put me down and do it gently." She tried to look indignant, but she was pretty sure all she did was look scared.

"Or what?" He smiled up at her. "You refused to believe me so I had to prove to you that my powers are real."

"Okay, so I believe you. Will you put me down?"

"I kinda like having you all nice and docile."

She didn't like the silkiness of his smile. It had to mean trouble. "Torin."

"Yes, Love?"

Her heart did a little flip when he called her *love*. "I don't want to fall."

"I promise you won't, but you'll have to trust me."

Could she trust him? She had given him her body. Why couldn't she

44

give him her trust?

~ * ~

Torin smiled when she slowly drifted down to the floor. He used her fear to hold the spell. The moment she started to trust him, the spell started to unravel. Now, of course, he could feel her anger, but he knew he had made some headway with her.

The moment her feet touched on the ground, she stalked over to him and punched his chest. "That was mean. You knew how I felt about falling, and you used it to get your way."

"And what would you do in my place?"

Stephanie scratched her head. "Okay, point taken. But next time, try not to scare me to death, okay?"

"You were never in danger. I would never let anything happen to you." He stepped up to her and traced the contour of her cheek. "You are far too precious."

She was the most important thing in his life. When it had happened, he wasn't sure. The bond between them grew stronger every hour. He could feel her emotions, the raw fear from dangling in the air had knifed through him. The look she gave him, combined with the emotions flowing through her squeezed at his heart.

He wondered if she could feel the bond yet. Did she understand she could feel his emotions? If she didn't, she would. The moment she could hear his thoughts in her head. Torin felt a shift in the calmness surrounding their hiding place. Someone was searching for them.

"Who do you think it is?" asked Stephanie as she stepped up to him, unconsciously seeking shelter from him.

She just answered his question for him.

"I believe it is your friend." He wrapped his arms around her. She felt good in his arms.

"He isn't my friend." Stephanie shivered. "And why would he be searching for us?"

"Because you ran from him?"

"I wish I hadn't heard something he didn't want repeated."

Anger started to boil in Torin. Wanting to hurt this woman because she happened to overhear something she shouldn't have didn't make sense.

"He had some plans that would hurt a lot of people. If I told the government, they could put him away for a long time. Mr. Tryst didn't want that to happen so he wanted to silence me."

"And still does." Torin took her hand and led her toward the back of the cave. "We need to get some more provisions."

"Why?"

"Because it looks like we're going to be staying here a little longer." He looked down into those beautiful eyes.

"This man isn't going to stop until he gets what he came for. He'll keep searching for me and will destroy everything in his path in the process." Stephanie laid a hand on his chest. "I have to go to him."

"No."

"Torin, he will start hurting the people in the village if I don't. Your people might not want to come here, but they know about this place, don't they?"

"Yes."

"Then Tryst will learn about it, too, and he won't think twice about invading your sanctuary."

He dropped his arms from around her and started pacing. "There are a few things I need before we allow him to take us."

"What is this 'us'? He doesn't want you, only me."

"Can't you feel it?" he asked softly. "We are bound to each other now. Our minds are becoming one. If he is determined to hurt you, he'll have to go through me to do it."

"Torin." She tilted her head up to look at him. The soft smile on her lips begged him to kiss her.

~ * ~

Stephanie felt her knees go weak when his lips touched hers. The potency of each kiss grew. If this kept up, pretty soon she'd incinerate from the heat of them. He always anticipated what she wanted. It was like he could read her mind.

I can.

She froze.

Torin sighed as he broke the kiss.

"You can hear me in your mind."

"No." It couldn't be true. If she could, she'd know… "How is this happening?"

"We are bonded."

She heard the regret in his voice, felt it in his mind. "What did you do?"

He didn't have to say anything. She knew. "How could you? No, don't answer, I already know, don't I? Oh of all the sneaky, underhanded things to do." She pulled her hand free of his grip. "And my righteous indignation does not make me sexier."

Stephanie turned back toward the water before he could give her that heart-melting smile of his. Dropping the blanket, she dove into the water and swam back under the waterfall. With the mind connection, she knew exactly where to go and what to avoid.

She reached the shoreline and searched for her clothes. She shoved her wet body into the dress, cursing and growling the whole time.

"I can't believe this. He used me. I've been through this before. I know better." Every time she said the word 'I', she stabbed herself in the chest. Hard.

"Stupid dress." She jerked the dress, and heard a tear, but finally the dress slid down her wet body.

"Nice show, my dear."

In that one instant, her rigid anger switched to fear. Tryst had found her.

Chapter Eight

Fear stabbed through Torin. "Stephanie."

He raced to the back of the cave. The secret passage would take him close to the path that led away from the waterfall. If he were quick enough, he'd be able to follow them.

As he climbed, he realized he never dressed. With one thought, he clothed himself.

Sunlight shot through the canopy, lighting his way as he climbed the last few meters to the forest floor. Hunching down near the ground, he listened for signs of their whereabouts.

"Tryst, these people," she said, looking at those who surrounded her. "Aren't going to follow you for very long. Once they know how slimy you truly are, they'll start fighting you."

"I can't believe you think so little of me, Miss Powers. I have already taken that precaution. I hold their leader and his family as hostages. With you by my side, they'll believe I control their precious wizard." Torin heard laughter. "They'll be too afraid to defy me."

Torin could feel Stephanie's revulsion.

They passed by his hiding place, in single file. Torin could snatch Stephanie as she passed him, but that wouldn't eliminate this man. Plus he had to have all the players together.

Closing his eyes, he searched for Tryst's partner. A grim smile spread across his face when he located him. His ticket to prison.

Torin sensed Stephanie's denial. She didn't want him to do what he planned. But he knew he had to be captured to be near her. They would conquer Tryst together, not apart.

Using a summonsing spell, Torin called the man to him. Time to finish the legend.

~ * ~

Stephanie wanted to throttle Torin. If he allowed himself to be captured, they'd be lost. Strands of the prophesy appeared in her head.

she will help defeat the evil that will invade
through the darkness she will see the truth

Torin, this can't be right. How can we defeat him as his prisoners? She feared for his safety.
The prophecy wouldn't lie to us, Stephanie. You must have faith.

She snorted. Right.

Tryst led the little troop of people back to the center of the small village, spouting off about how he planned on getting rid of her before returning home to continue his quest for nuclear arms.

Stephanie wondered why he wasn't on his litter. He sure looked like he enjoyed having people carrying him around the last time.

If she had a BB gun and a few pebbles, she could try to knock some sense into the man. A slingshot would even do nicely. And maybe he'd shut up if she whacked him on the head a couple of times.

She'd at least feel better.

"What are you smiling about, Miss Powers?" His words cut into her daydreaming.

"Nothing you'd be interested in, Mr. Tryst."

"Try me."

"I was wondering if you were ever going to shut up. You keep talking and talking, but I haven't seen any action."

He moved so quickly, he had her by the throat before she could react.

"Never underestimate me, Miss Powers. I always do what I set out to do." His fingers squeezed her throat, cutting the air off.

Dots started to appear in front of her eyes.

"Do you understand me?"

49

She nodded.

"Good." He released her throat and continued on with his litany.

Stephanie staggered when he released her. She massaged her throat, knowing she'd probably end up with bruises from that.

Their little entourage slowed as they neared the clearing.

"Well, well, what have we here?" Tryst sounded a little too happy for Stephanie's taste.

She walked up to the edge of the small group and groaned silently. There sat Torin with a rifle pointed at his head. He looked up at her and winked.

She wanted to kill him.

"I heard you were looking for this guy, Boss." Jolly kept the rifle aimed at Torin's head.

"Very good, Mr. Jolly. Our wizard can join Miss Powers. You, come walk with me."

Torin stepped up to where Stephanie stood.

"That was stupid," she whispered.

"It had to be done."

"And what if he decides to kill us right away?" she asked softly. "Where's your prophecy if Mr. Tryst won't play along?"

"He will." Torin touched her on the arm. To anyone else it looked like harmless contact. Stephanie felt the energy he released into her body. Suddenly, she was filled with happiness and well-being, and she felt loved.

As they approached the small village, the people peeked out of their windows. Stephanie could hear their shocked whispers when they spotted Torin. They probably thought the great wizard had fallen.

Tryst stopped their small entourage in front of the largest house in the village. Of course, he would commandeer it for himself.

"Put them in the caves," Tryst said.

No one moved toward Torin.

Stephanie couldn't help but smile. Tryst might not believe Torin was any danger to him, but the people knew better, and they didn't want to face his wrath.

"Mr. Jolly, take them." Tryst gave directions then turned on the villagers. "You defy me? Who would like to join your wizard?"

The crowd shrank back. Stephanie noticed the little girl who had been at Torin's house earlier that day. Tears streaked her face.

Poor thing. Bet she thought she was doing a good thing when she announced Stephanie's presence. She couldn't have known what Tryst would do.

Jolly led them around the corner of the house and down a path. One of the villagers who had been assigned to guard the house, stiffened as they went by.

"You! Follow me."

Stephanie watched the silent communication between Torin and the man before he obeyed Jolly.

"Do you know where he is taking us?" she whispered.

Use your mind to talk to me, Stephanie.

This isn't natural for me, she responded.

I know, but it is for our safety now. Torin paused for a moment. *Jolly is leading us toward a group of caves under the village. They are used in emergencies.*

Then they're not designed to hold prisoners?

No. There are no cages, like the ones I see in your mind. We don't have criminals here, like you do in your world.

Then why are we going?

So the villagers won't be hurt by Tryst, and to fulfill the prophecy. Remember, Tryst was named in the prophecy too.

A few more strands of the prophecy filtered through her mind.

but jokester and teasers will abound
and refusing to give any ground

Jolly led them around to the mouth of the first cave.

"No. We need to be in the third one," said Torin.

Stephanie wanted to know why, but kept her thoughts to herself. Besides, Torin would probably just smile and say remember the prophecy.

The guard, though, didn't argue with him.

Stephanie couldn't help but shake her head. Tryst didn't understand how these people felt about Torin. *And you're betting on that, aren't you?*

Once the guard was sure they were safely inside the cave, he turned away and stood at the mouth.

Torin took her hand and led her deeper into the cave. Urged her to sit on the sandy ground, then crouched down beside her. "Stephanie, do you remember the prophecy?"

"Yeah, for some strange reason I do." She looked at him. "I think this little link of ours has something to do with that."

"What did it tell us to do?"

"Something about right is wrong and wrong is right."

He grasped her hands. "What does that mean to you?"

"I don't know. That we should go left instead of right?"

"All right. Now, what is the right thing to do in this situation?"

"Stop him?" She didn't know where these questions were headed, but right now they were giving her a headache.

"How?"

She didn't know.

"How about my magic?"

"But would that be right?" She paused as the words sank in. "Oh. Right is wrong and wrong is right."

"It's not really your battle, but mine. Although you could defeat him, I am the one who must confront him."

Torin smiled. "One more question."

"What?" She looked at him curiously. So many questions.

"What about *your* magic?"

"I don't have any magic." She laughed at that one.

"Oh?"

"Oh, what?" Stephanie stood back up. "I don't have a magical bone in my body."

"I want to show you something." Torin stood up and went to the mouth of the cave. He lured the guard back to where Stephanie sat. Once again, he created a ball of energy. Looking at the guard he asked, "Would you like to hold this?"

"But—" After hesitating for a moment, he held out his hands. Torin placed the ball into the man's hand. It immediately sunk into his palm and broke apart.

Torin created another ball and held it out to Stephanie, who took it and held it in the palm of her hand without a problem.

The young guard dropped to his knees. "She is like you."

"He's crazy."

"You are holding the energy ball, are you not?"

"Sure, but—"

"No mortal can hold any illusion a wizard conjures up. Only another wizard can."

"No." She backed away from him.

"It's true, Stephanie."

"It can't be."

"What are you afraid of?" Torin took a step toward her. She took another back.

"I'm normal."

"I didn't say you weren't. But you are a wizard."

Stephanie shook her head. All those years, she had been labeled as weird. Different. And how she had hated it. Now, when she had finally put it all behind her, it reared its ugly head again.

"You have a very special gift."

"Yeah? What about you? Your neighbors shun you, except when they need something from you. They fear you. Treat you like a leper. I don't want that." She whispered the last part. "Not again."

"You are wrong. I cultivated their attitude. There was no one to teach me how to control my powers. I could look at someone crossly, and they'd end up with donkey ears. Until I could control my powers, I kept them away from me, not the other way around."

"Then why was that woman afraid of you? Of the prophesy?" Stephanie asked.

"Think about it. Her daughter was eight years old. She needed her at home, helping with the chores. Any child destined to be my bride would be pampered and spoiled. It wasn't me she was afraid of, but being alone. She just didn't express it very well."

Stephanie frowned. Okay, so what he said made sense. But she didn't have to like it.

"You have the power, embrace it."

"No

Chapter Nine

Torin didn't know what to do. She had to accept her gifts. If she refused them, she could lose them. He didn't understand her fear of the magic. It made him wonder what she went through as a child to make her react this way. "Tell me why."

Stephanie sighed. He watched as she started to pace, not quite sure where to begin.

"When I was little, I could make things happen."

He nodded. Not unusual for someone with their gifts.

"Everyone called me jinx because I was always there when someone got hurt. I knew I caused the accidents. They always happened to people who had just made fun of me or hurt my feelings." Stephanie looked up at him with pain-filled eyes. "It got to a point where no one would talk to me. They were afraid of what might happen if they got too close."

The sadness on her face struck him to the core.

"Then one day it just stopped."

"You gained control of your anger."

She looked at him. "Why did you say that?"

"If you didn't get angry at your friends for teasing you then they wouldn't get hurt."

"How did you know that?"

"I went through the same thing." He smiled at her. "But you still have the power. You just never tapped it."

"I wouldn't know how."

"I can show you. It's very easy." He stood up and offered his hand. At first, he thought she would say no, but then he saw her hesitant nod.

Stephanie turned out to be a fast learner. Torin was amazed at how quickly she picked up his teachings.

"This is so cool."

"You're a quick study. Can you mimic anything I do?"

"I'm not sure. I can try."

"Good." He smiled. "Then it's time to go and find our little friend Mr. Tryst."

~ * ~

Stephanie followed Torin through the cave, hoping he knew the way out. She was so confused; she knew she'd be lost forever. He stopped when they came to a fork in the passageway.

"So? Which way do we go?"

"Um, I'm not sure." He looked one way then the other before he turned toward her and gave her a sheepish smile.

"What?" Stephanie put her hands on her hips. "I don't believe this. You, the great wizard, can't remember which way to go?"

"Well, I've never been this way before." He looked both ways again. "Which way would you go?"

"I don't know. The right?" She looked to the right. "Make that the left."

"Why?"

"It just feels better. That right is wrong, and wrong is right."

She felt his smile more than saw it. The cave turned and twisted its way up into the back of a small cottage.

"Where are we?" she whispered.

"Right behind Mr. Tryst," he whispered back.

Stephanie nodded as she spotted the man. The moment she saw the people kneeling in front of Tryst's chair with their heads bowed and their hands tied, she forgot all reason and started forward. Torin's restraining hand on her shoulder brought her back to reality.

We must be cautious. They don't know we're here yet. Let's use that to our advantage.

How?

Watch and learn. Torin took her hand and led her into the center of the room. They now stood between Tryst and the kneeling people.

Why don't they see us?

Because we're cloaked. It makes for a grand entrance when you want to show off.

And we want to show off?

Of course.

"Why have you disobeyed me?" asked Tryst.

The people before him just kept their heads hung. Stephanie wasn't sure if it was fear or humiliation they felt at this point.

Tryst sighed as he stood up. "I really have tried to be patient with you. I didn't ask for much, yet you refuse me at every turn." He stepped within inches of where Torin and Stephanie stood.

"So what do you want to do about it, Boss?" asked Mr. Jolly.

Tryst turned toward his partner. If he could see them, he would be staring directly into Torin's face. "Kill them."

"I think not," said Torin as he grabbed Tryst's hand. He mentally urged Stephanie to do the same thing with Jolly.

Tryst had no clue what had grabbed him, but he fought like a madman to get it off him. The moment Stephanie had a hold on Jolly, Torin let them materialize.

Jolly fainted at Stephanie's feet.

Tryst turned as white as a sheet. "Wh-where did you come from?"

"Thin air." Torin gave him a sly grin, one that sent chills down Stephanie's spine. "What have these people done to warrant death?"

Tryst didn't answer him, he just stared at Torin. "How did you do that? Mirrors?"

"What is it about your world that you don't believe in magic?" Torin sounded exasperated. "I am a wizard. I can conjure things."

"No one can do that," mumbled Tryst.

"Oh? How do you explain what just happened here? Your friend fainted because of it." Torin looked at one of the guards standing there. "Bind that fool before he wakes up."

Stephanie was glad to relinquish her hold on Jolly. Now she could help Torin when needed.

"A trick."

"It's no trick," said Stephanie.

"Hah. You want me to believe you?" Tryst tried to break Torin's hold once more. "I have seen better magicians."

"You really don't want to make Torin angry." She stepped up to his side. "He's uncontrollable when he's angry."

"Love, I'm not that bad." Torin never took his eyes off Tryst.

"So he says," said Stephanie. "He's very protective of this village. If anyone's been harmed, well, I feel sorry for you."

One of the people who had been kneeling whispered. "He hurt Mother Abigail, and we don't know where Father Norah is."

Through her link with Torin, Stephanie knew the two were the leaders of this village.

Torin started to draw energy into himself. Through their mental link, he shared his skill with her then asked her to do the same. The sensation was euphoric.

Slowly, Tryst rose in the air until his feet hung several inches off the ground.

"Put me down!"

Torin ignored the squalls of the man. He concentrated on Stephanie instead.

"Remember the ball of energy?" At her nod, he continued. "We need to build one like it."

"We?"

"You can do this, Stephanie. Open your mind."

She closed her eyes and cleared her mind of any wayward thoughts.

"Good. Now picture the ball of energy in front of you, your hands forging it into a bright blue ball."

Energy leapt from her fingertips. It swayed and dipped before she felt another source blended with hers. Torin had joined his powers with hers. She felt the ball take shape, growing large enough to encompass the two men. The energy field fluctuated then became solid.

A giggle escaped her. The energy flowing through and around her made her feel invincible.

"Careful, Love." Torin continued to shape the energy ball, adding his power to it. "You'll find it very taxing on the body. Don't drain yourself."

A few more bursts of energy and she could tell it was completed. She opened her eyes.

"Wow."

Tryst saw the ball and started to squirm. "You can't do this."

"Oh, I can. Think of me as the warrior of this village. Most of the time I heal and keep my magic private, but I am here whenever my people need me." Torin directed the ball toward Tryst. "You have violated our laws, brought anger and despair to a peaceful village. Our laws are quite clear. Death, or sentencing by the wizard. Which would you prefer?"

Tryst swallowed hard. Stephanie didn't think he liked either option.

"It is painless." The ball drew closer to Tryst, tearing a scream out of the man. Stephanie thought he screamed like a girl. His scream continued until the ball swallowed the sound. He floated motionless inside the ball.

"What will happen to him?"

"It is like your, um." He searched her mind for the right word. "Cryogenics. He's frozen in there."

The guards threw Mr. Jolly inside the ball as well.

"They will remain there until I release them." He faced the ball and opened his arms. Slowly he brought them together. The ball shrank as his arms closed toward each other until the ball was no larger than a marble.

"And what happens if he escapes?"

"He can't." Torin pulled the small ball toward his hand then closed his fingers around it when it landed in his palm. Stephanie heard him mumble a few words before the ball winked out of sight.

"Where'd it go?"

"A safe place, I promise." He took her hand and led her out of the building.

"What about the villagers?"

"They will do better without me hovering around. When they are ready, they will come to speak to us."

"Us?" Stephanie's voice squeaked.

"You will stay with me, won't you?"

"I have a life back there, Torin. One I worked hard to create. I can't just walk away from it."

He nodded. "You do what's best."

"That's it? You're not going to beg me to stay?" Why wasn't he

58

fighting to keep her?

"Would it do me any good?"

She shook her head.

Torin escorted her to the cave that led to her world. "Understand that when you leave, there can be no turning back. The doorway that allowed you to come here might not reappear if you change your mind."

"Come with me."

"I can't, Stephanie. The village needs me."

She felt torn. Go back to what she had before, or stay here and create a whole new life. What was more important now? The prestige she felt as CEO of Power Imaging or her love for Torin? What would Mia expect of her.

Stephanie looked longingly at the cave then at Torin. "I need to go back."

He nodded again. Were those tears she saw in his eyes?

"To tell my friends I won't be back."

He grabbed her and hugged her tight. "You don't have to leave here. You're a wizard remember?"

"Don't tell me I can be in two places at the same time."

"No, but you can project yourself so you can visit your friends in your world from time to time. I can show you how to do this."

"And what will you charge me if I hire you to train me?" she asked.

He wiggled his eyebrows at her. "Oh, I'm sure I can think of something."

THE END

Crystals and Disappearing Cats

Chapter One

"And now back to our special *The Wizard of Oz*."

"Nope. Not for this girl." Glenda grabbed the remote and clicked the TV off. "I've had enough of *Glenda the Good Witch* to last me a life time."

Silence wrapped her in a cocoon as she headed to the kitchen. She had a few dishes to clean before she had to face the box that arrived this morning. Her inheritance. "I'm sure going to miss you, Grandma."

Too quickly, she found herself sitting in front of the medium-sized brown box with a steak knife in her hand. It didn't look like much but she knew it held precious parts of her grandmother's life. Opening it broke her heart, her grief was still very raw, but she needed to move past the death of her grandmother. Grandma wouldn't want her to mourn but celebrate her life.

Her heart constricted when she sliced through the tape and pulled back the flaps. A sigh escaped her when she found the box lined with several sets of sheets. Good old mom. Instead of using newspaper like normal people, she used things her daughter might need. Like she didn't know how to buy these things herself.

Moving aside a couple of the sheets, she found bundles. Whatever grandma had left, her Mom had wrapped them in some sort of cloth. "Oh come on, Mom, shirts? Do I not know how to clothe myself?"

The first package she opened revealed an old Stief teddy bear. It was missing one eye and some of its felt, but she felt all warm and fuzzy inside as she remembered playing with this bear at her grandma's house.

Each gift brought back a beautiful memory. Some brought tears to her eyes. She knew she'd be pulling each out later to enjoy again. The last item she pulled out was a small velvet box. A frown creased her brow. Opening the box, she found a crystal pendant. What was this? A Christmas present? It sure wasn't familiar. Just as she was going to call her mom and ask about it, she found a yellowed piece of paper tucked in the lid.

Dearest granddaughter,

This heirloom has been passed down from grandmothers to granddaughters for generations. It isn't for the lighthearted. It can grant your heart's desire. It can also make your worst dreams come true. Be careful when you wear it, to lose it at the wrong time will be your undoing. May all your wishes come true.

Glenda flipped the paper around. No signature. "Very weird."
She looked at the clock. "Oh crap! I've got to get ready."
Glenda faced her first date in about four months and he was due in less than an hour. After racing through her shower and applying her makeup in record time, she stared at her closet, wondering what she should wear. First dinner in a nice restaurant then a stand up comedy show. She ended up wearing a pair of black slacks with a silk pink blouse. Not too dressy or too desperate.

The doorbell rang before she could decide on jewelry. All she had in sight was the crystal necklace and her simple gold hoops. Grabbing them, she headed toward the door. "That'll have to do."

~ * ~

It didn't take her very long to figure out the date was a mistake. Her date Brian did nothing but laugh at his own jokes and tell her how much 'stuff' he had. She wasn't sure if she could handle much more. Excusing herself, she went to the bathroom to get a little reprieve.

Her reflection stared back at her. The crystal bounced softly against her soft silk shirt. "Watch what I wish for, huh? This is the one time I wish I had the power to change my life. I want adventure and true love and I won't find it with these men my friends keep setting me up with. I wish I could leave here and leave all the cares of life behind."

She felt the crystal grow warm against her chest. At first, she thought the light in the bathroom caught in its facets, making the necklace glow but when it grew so bright she couldn't see anything else she knew something strange was going on. The light overpowered her senses.

Her world disappeared.

Heat infused her body. She felt like she floated in the air. Wind started to wrap around her body, picking up speed and tightening around her. Breathing became difficult. What was happening to her?

The heat lessened and the wind softened, allowing her to catch her breath. Still blinded by the light pouring out of the crystal, Glenda thought it didn't seem to be as intense as before.

She started to make out shapes as time went on. *Trees?* She didn't remember trees in the bathroom. The images became clearer. *Uh oh. This wasn't the bathroom. Where was she?*

Looking around, she found herself in a forest. This new setting confused her even more. Instead of nighttime, it was now late afternoon. How did she get there? The small path she found herself on went in to two different directions. Which way to go? Something told her to go east and standing in the middle of the forest wasn't an option.

Her feet took her to a small cluster of homes. They looked like something out of the dark ages, more hovels than anything livable did. A few people milled about in the small clearing centered between the houses. Maybe they'd be willing to help. "Um, excuse me."

Several of the people turned toward her and gasped. Within seconds, they were prostrate on the ground.

Barbara Donlon Bradley

What was going on? Was this how they greeted all strangers? "Please? I need someone's help."

"Perhaps I can be of assistance?" a deep male voice said.

All she saw was the top of his head because he bowed in front of her "Yes. I'm…"

"We know who you are, G'Linda. We have been waiting for you. Your rooms are ready. If you'll follow me?" He took a couple of steps before turning around to be sure she was coming.

The way he said her name was a little strange but it could have been his accent. It was different then anything she had ever heard. She didn't know where she was or who any of these people were but they knew her for some reason. Maybe following him could lead to answers. She mumbled to herself, "Why not?"

He walked through the small village and followed a narrow path into another wooded area.

Where was he taking her? "Look, maybe I should go back."

"I'm sorry. Have I done wrong? Your instructions said you wanted to be away from the village but be able to see everything that goes on. The only location we have to fit your request is up there." He pointed up an incline.

Was she dreaming? How about some sort of illusion? All she knew was she'd gone this far. He seemed harmless enough, and she had no other place to go. "You have not done wrong."

He seemed placated with that. "It's not much farther, and I promise you'll love the view."

She nodded. They continued to climb up the hill to the top. A cute little thatched roof home overlooked the valley were the village nestled. Looked like something out of a fairy tale.

"Your new home." He bowed and waited for her to move.

What was she supposed to do now? Wait for him to open the door, reach for it herself? She didn't know.

~ * ~

G'Linda didn't act the way he expected. The stories he heard had him fearing the worst. He heard she was a dragon, demanding everything and respecting nothing. The woman who stood before him seemed very

66

lost and confused. Stepping up to the door, he opened it and bowed as she stepped inside.

"Do you have a name?" she asked as she passed by him and into the house.

"Ah, yes. D'Eric." He hadn't expected that. From what he learned, she didn't want to know anyone's name.

His brother's village had summoned her several years ago when they were attacked by the wendibeast. She had been horrible to them but the spell to get rid of the beast worked and he had heard stories like this from other villages. Her magic was strong. She might be hard to live with but she cured the problem at hand.

Their problem had terrorized them for a while and could destroy the village. He had to appease her to save his people.

"This is great." She pushed her hands into two small slits in the front of her pants and bounced on her heels.

Her clothing was a bit unorthodox but he was warned to not react to anything she said or did. "We hoped you would like it."

"Well I do. So you can go home now."

Was she testing him? Another thing he had been told was to never leave her alone. Her demands came to her on a whim and if there were no one there to hear them there would be hell to pay. "I'm here to serve."

She looked disappointed. She patted her finger against her lips as she thought. He couldn't take his eyes off of the movement. Her lips were luscious. Full, pouty and very kissable. The vibrant red couldn't be natural but it called to him. Begging him to caress them.

"You okay?" She frowned at him.

She must have sensed where his thoughts had gone. He dropped his gaze to the floor. "Yes. Of course. I could make a refreshment for you if you please."

"That would be fine." She wandered around the small house, taking it all in as he grabbed a pitcher and started working on her drink.

He watched her out of the corner of his eye as she picked up a bauble here or there. When she ran her fingers against the polished surface, he wished it were his body she caressed.

Oh, he had to get his mind back on his task before he did something wrong and she caught him. He had heard the stories of her anger. "Your drink is ready."

"Thank you." She took the drink he offered and took a sip. Her face lit up as the flavors seeped into her taste buds. "This is wonderful."

He gave her a slight bow.

"Aren't you going to have any?" She set her glass down when she noticed him empty-handed. G'Linda moved to the counter he had stood at and picked up the pitcher. She peered into the container before setting it down and rummaging around for something. She was very intent in her search as she lifted curtains and opened doors. "Isn't there another glass or cup here?"

"I'll go get one right now." He started to the door but stopped when he felt the heat of her hand on his arm.

"That's okay." She left the glass on the table and moved to the window. "So I guess you'll be going now?"

"I'm here to do your bidding." He bowed again.

"Then I bid you good bye." She gave him a bright smile as she walked to the door and opened it.

He stayed in his bow but looked up at her. What was she up to now? Why was she trying so hard to get rid of him? "Excuse me?"

"You don't need to stay."

"But, what if you need something?" What else could he say? Her reaction was so far off what he had been told he couldn't stop the words from slipping from his mouth.

~ * ~

What would it take to get this man to leave? She needed to get back to the wooded area where she first showed up and see if she could find a way home and his presence hampered that intention. "I promise to not need anything until the morning."

He didn't seem to like her answer. "I can't."

A sigh escaped her. Somehow, she had to get some time alone. But how? This guy was like a bulldog. She couldn't seem to shake him. "So what am I supposed to do now?"

"Nothing. This time is yours."

"Then I need some time to myself to prepare." He stared at her with such hopeful eyes. It made her feel like a heel, but she had to get out of here.

"Of course." He walked over to one of the closed doors and opened it. "You may meditate in here if you like."

Glenda stepped into paradise. The huge four-poster bed caught her eye first with its overflowing amount of silk pillows and gauze drapes. This was a little girl's fantasy. Who was she kidding? This was her fantasy too. All she needed was a nice hunky man. Like her bow and scraper, what was his name? Derek? She wouldn't kick him out of her bed.

He had a very nice physique. What she could see despite the robe-like outfit he wore. It left a lot to the imagination, but she had a good one. His muscled arms showed he worked for a living, not sculpted them in a gym somewhere. His deep brown eyes had little flecks of green and gold. She could stare at them all day.

She grinned. Her train of thought would distract her from using this little bit of time alone. How she was going to use it she wasn't sure, but hoped something would come to her once he was on the other side of the door. "Thank you."

He just stood there. This was not good.

"You need to leave the room now." Since he didn't seem to take a subtle hint, maybe being blunt would do the trick.

"Of course." He bowed again and left the room.

What was with the bowing anyway? She didn't get it. Turning her back to the door, she focused on how she got here. Somehow, she had left the bathroom of the restaurant and ended up near this small village. How? She wasn't sure, but if she was fantasizing this it was the best fantasy she ever had. Everything was tactile. She could feel the wood of the furniture, the soft linen of the tablecloths. It seemed too real to be a dream.

So what should she do? Her first instinct was to go back to where she appeared to find whatever opening allowed her to come here. The sooner the better. But her personal bower wouldn't let her out of his sight. Except for now. She took one look at the door and knew this was probably her only chance to leave undetected. Now she had to figure out how to get out of the house. The window near her bed beckoned. "Oh this isn't a smart move."

She lifted the window and looked around. The ground outside the window was clean and level. This she could do without getting hurt. Climbing up on the windowsill, Glenda rolled up her pants so she could swing her legs over the sill without a hitch. With one leg out the window and the other bent up to slip through, she heard the bedroom door open.

Why didn't she lock that stupid door?

Chapter Two

What was she doing? D'Eric stared at her in shock. "Did you need to get somewhere?"

She looked at him like a child who got caught stealing a sweet. Then she started to laugh. A beautiful melodious sound that pierced him straight in the heart. "What has caught your humor?"

She laughed a little harder. "You mean tickled my funny bone? I guess getting caught climbing out my window like a teen-ager made me realize how crazy this whole idea was. I wanted to return to where I first arrived."

"Why?" The twinkle in her eyes made him want to do anything for her, and he would as long as she kept that look in her eye.

"I lost something and would like to find it." She pulled her leg back in the window. "The way you've been shadowing me I was afraid you'd stop me from going back."

"I will escort you." He bowed and gestured for her to precede him.

"Must you bow so much?"

He stopped in his tracks. "That is how I show you respect."

"And I appreciate it, but it's a little disconcerting." She didn't have the heart to tell him she was tired of looking at the top of his head.

"As you wish." He gestured for her to go first.

"And I have no clue where I'm going. I'd rather follow." She thought he was going to have a seizure for a moment before he gave her a slight nod. A smile flirted with her lips as he hesitantly lead her out of the house and down the path to the village. He stopped where he met her and turned to face her.

Okay so now she had to figure out where she came from. She was pretty sure she had followed the path into the village, so she walked toward the small copse of trees behind it. Was this where she appeared? She had no clue.

She had to walk backwards. Maybe that would help. The first images of this strange place were burned into her mind. Turning to face them, she wanted to laugh at their expressions. It had to look crazy. But she had to focus. Looking around, she got her bearings. She was farther back on the trail when she first got here.

One foot behind the other, she continued to back up. It took only a few more steps, and she stood at the spot where she first realized she was no longer in the bathroom of the restaurant.

Now what?

She was trying to figure out what to do next when Derrick shuffled toward her. The bow was back. He wanted something. "Yes?"

"We must return soon, G'Linda. It's not safe to be out in the dark."

Oh, great. He's afraid of the dark. She didn't have time for this. "Look, it's okay. Why don't you head back to the house and I'll catch up in a few minutes."

A small crowd gathered around him. Like Derrick, they seemed agitated at the sight of the setting sun. Several kept looking between her and the woods before peering nervously toward their small homes.

A sigh escaped her. She didn't want to anger the people. They'd be angry enough when they found out she wasn't whom they thought. "Let's go. I can come back tomorrow."

The sigh was communal. Obviously, they were very happy with her answer.

She shook her head as she followed Derrick back toward the house. He picked up the pace to an almost run as the sun dipped lower and lower in the sky. Vibrant colors of crimson, yellow, and orange ribboned the sky. It was beautiful. Too bad she couldn't enjoy it. The house came into view just as the sun slid behind the horizon. His gesture was frantic. What was freaking these people out?

The solid click of the door behind her filled the silence once she entered the house. "So are you going to explain why everyone's acting so crazy?"

He gave her an odd look. "Crazy?"

"Is everyone racing to get indoors before the sun sets normal for you guys?"

His head nodded once. "For the last three months it has been. It's why we sent for you."

Good. Some information. Glenda wondered if she would ever get an idea why they had sent for the person she was pretending to be. Lying to them didn't sit right, but who would believe she came from ...where? A different time? Another dimension? How about another planet? Any of them would explain so much, but which one was right? And asking Derrick the wrong questions could be detrimental. So what should she do? Damn Grandma and her crystal.

Derrick headed straight to the kitchen. "Are you hungry? I can whip up something quickly."

"Sure." Would they speak the same way if she were on another planet? Glenda was pretty sure they wouldn't be able to communicate if they were from two different worlds, no matter what the science fiction shows showed. Plus the sunset looked pretty normal. If she had been on another planet, wouldn't the sky be different? Maybe she could sneak outside and check out the stars. If he would let her.

Derrick also spoke like everyone else from her world.

"I have a nice stew that has been simmering all day. I hope you like it." He spooned some of the soup into a small wooden bowl and placed it on the table. After setting a wooden spoon next to the bowl, he filled the leather cup with water and put that with the rest.

Glenda sat down and picked up the spoon. "Did you get another set?"

"Yes." He pointed to a small sack she hadn't noticed. "I asked one of the people to go to my home and bring everything I need."

"Good. Then get some food and join me." She scooped up some of the stew on her spoon.

"Are you sure?"

She had already stuffed the spoon into her mouth so all she could do was nod. Eating alone was not one of her favorite things to do; so she sure hoped he didn't do something crazy like go outside and eat in the bushes. A smile eased across her lips as he set his plate on the table. He started to eat standing up.

"What are you doing?"

"There is no chair."

Glenda looked around. He was right. "Fine." She stood and picked up her plate. "Then we can sit on the floor."

He gave her a confused look but picked up his bowl and followed suit. "This is most unusual."

"I know but we have a lack of chairs." She grinned before continuing to eat. "Think of it as a picnic indoors."

He nodded and picked up his bowl. "Tomorrow I will make sure we have two of the things two people would normally share in a situation like this."

"Thank you." A strange noise outside made her turn her head. Hearing nothing else, she brushed it off as her imagination taking a normal noise and blowing it all out of proportion.

A nearby roar wasn't as easy to ignore. "That wasn't familiar. What kind of animal is it?"

"That is why we hired you." He said it so matter-of-factly she knew he believed every word he said.

Glenda choked on her food. "Excuse me?"

"You know. Like you did for other villages?" He must have noticed her deer in the headlight look because he continued. "When you caused one of the village's crops to grow after a bad drought? Or helped the villagers that had the problem with the vermin? You helped get rid of their problem, too. Shall I go on?"

Was that what this other Glenda did? Traveled from town to town and cured the town's problems for profit? Was she some sort of charlatan or a true miracle worker?

What had she gotten herself into?

It took a second or two for her to realize she should answer. "Of course. But I need more information on the creature. Has anyone seen it?"

"The only people who have seen it are the ones who died." He scooped up stew and popped it into his mouth.

That was an important bit of information. Don't get too close just to get a look at it. It could be detrimental to your health. "What can you tell me about it then?"

"No one has ever been attacked during the day so we feel it's a nocturnal beast. It's never attacked in the heart of the village either. It might be afraid of crowds." He placed the spoon into the bowl.

Instinct probably kept it to the outskirts of the town where it picked off one person at a time. "Does it happen at any particular time of the evening?"

"Good question. I'd have to talk to the villagers to be sure but I think the attacks all happened before most went to bed for the evening."

"And the attacks always happened outside?" She stirred her food while she thought. Was it intelligent? "This creature has never jumped through a window or crashed through a door?"

"No. The call went out when someone was missing. It took several killings before we realized we were being stalked by something."

"It must live nearby." She tapped her finger against her lips. "How long has this been going on?"

"You ask very good questions. About three months."

"It's a gift." She didn't have the heart to tell him she did this for a living as a reporter for her local paper. Fluff pieces were more her style but asking the right questions came naturally. "How many people have been killed?"

"Six." He picked up his bowl and started eating again. The subject must be exhausted. Derrick at least seemed to be over it.

At least she had something to work with. What she would do with it was a different story. In the morning, she'd talk to some of the people. Maybe one of them would be able to shed a little light on some of the fuzzier areas.

They finished their meals in silence. Derrick picked up the bowls and took them to the kitchen. After he cleaned them up, he stacked them to the side. "If you wish to rest for the night you can go ahead. This won't take me very long."

Glenda thought his comment a little odd but nodded. She figured it was a courtesy for everyone to retire at the same time. The bedroom windows were open, letting the calm breeze flow through. The soft sounds of the night soothed her.

As she prepared for bed, the creature roared. She jumped about two feet when she heard it. It sounded too close. Like the creature was right outside the window. Instinct had her running from the windows; then she remembered that, according to villagers' reports, the creature never gained access through a window. She should be safe.

She hoped.

A linen gown rested against the covers. A smile spread on her face as she removed her outfit. The gown slid down her body. A little see through but very comfortable. She slid between the sheets, still smiling. She sure could get used to this. The soft tick down of the bed relaxed her in seconds. In minutes, she was asleep.

Her peace was broken moments later, when the bed dipped. The warmth of another body brought her awake instantly. She didn't think, just acted and grabbed the nearest limb. It felt like an arm. One tug and she flipped whoever was trying to get into her bed over her head. The body attached to the arm landed on the floor with a thud.

A very male groan filled the air. "G'Linda?"

"Derrick?" She peered over the edge of the bed to find a very startled and very naked man.

Holy cow, what a magnificent body. She backed up a little on the bed because she was afraid her rampant drool would drip onto his body. Goodness, he didn't have just a six-pack but an entire case. His muscular arms hadn't given her a hint of all the muscles on his body.

She had found him attractive when she first met him. Add the body and he was a dream come true and he was naked at her feet.

"Why did you attack me?" He sounded offended.

"Sorry. I was asleep and didn't expect company." She sat back in the bed. "I forgot this was the only bed."

"I am only following your orders."

"Mine?" What else did this Glenda ask for? A boy toy? "I think you should go over my requests again. Just to make sure you have covered everything."

"Of course." He sat up and crossed his legs to make himself more comfortable. "You requested a home overlooking the village, a servant to care for your meals and basic needs."

She must have missed the basic needs part earlier. "So you are to please me in every way? No matter what I need?"

76

"Every desire."

Every desire? Wow. Her mind raced at the thoughts that leaped to life. He was hers; he would do anything she wanted. But could she? Taking advantage of Derrick wasn't right. At least she'd never do it in her world. But she wasn't in her world. She was here and here he was, ready, willing and able.

Chapter Three

"Perhaps a little massage will help relax you."

She didn't realize she was tense until he spoke. Knowing she could ask anything of him freaked her out just a little. Jumping into bed with a stranger was a foreign thing to her.

Her lack of a sex life had a lot to do with it. Glenda could count on one hand how many men she had been with. One was her high school boyfriend, who matched her level of inexperience. Their first time turned out to be a night of disappointment. Virginity gone but no great love story to share with her friends. The next opportunity was in college and she was too drunk to remember what happened. Then there were the other brief, unsatisfying experiences with two other men she dated. After four tries, she gave up.

A massage was nice and safe. Right? Something she could handle. "Okay."

"Good." He climbed up on the bed. Kneeling, he placed his hands on his thighs, a gesture that gave her a very safe feeling even though he was naked. "Lay on your stomach."

She blinked at him before moving. Glenda was glad he gave her direction because otherwise she simply would have sat and stared at his nakedness. Flipping over, she snuggled into the softness of the bed again.

Derrick worked the gown off her shoulders, moving it to her waistline. He placed his hands on her shoulders and kneaded them slowly. "Relax."

How could she relax when she felt his naked body straddling hers? The flimsy gown she wore left nothing to the imagination. It took all her will power not to grab him by the leg and drag him down with her.

Then her mind took off.

She imagined him kneeling at her feet, ready to do her bidding. What an image. What would she ask of him first?

A moan escaped her when he worked on one section of her back. "That feels so good."

Maybe she'd get him to do exactly what he did now. He sure had an art to it. The tightness in her muscles melted under his ministrations. Oh, yeah. This was the life. "This is wonderful."

"I'm glad you're enjoying it." He pressed his weight against the small of her back, wringing another groan from her. He worked down her back, kneading, and massaging then moved to her legs.

She felt boneless. When he urged her to roll over again she didn't resist. His hands felt too good and she didn't want him to stop.

He continued to massage her, starting with her feet before working up to her ankles, calves, knees, and thighs. The gentle movement relaxed her so much she was on the verge of sleep.

A hand brushed against her breasts, drawing a sigh from her. Feather-like fingertips stroked her collarbone, the inside of her arms, across her hip. It made her feel soft, sexy and loved. She didn't want him to stop.

"I hope I'm not being too bold."

"Shhh. No words to break the spell you weave." She pressed her fingers against his lips, not wanting to break the fantasy she was creating for herself. "Tonight I will let you have control, but only if you keep silent."

She closed her eyes and let herself go, let the sensations wash over her. The softness of his fingers, the heat of his breath, the press of his body, everything seemed more intense.

Her body shuttered when she felt his lips on her neck for the first time. It was gentle, just a light touch against her throat but she felt it to her core. His lips blazed a blistering trail to her breast, setting her blood afire along the way.

Any sex she had before was a lot of groping and grunting. Now she felt like she was being worshiped. He paid alms to her body, making her feel precious, cherished.

It brought tears to her eyes.

Derrick paused in his ministrations for a moment and Glenda feared she had done something wrong. Then she felt his tongue licking away her tears. His reaction made more spill.

"If you keep crying we'll never get anywhere." His voice, nothing more than a whisper, brushed against her ears.

Laughter bubbled up inside her. She couldn't stop the sound from escaping. A soft lyrical sound filled the room. That couldn't be her. Her laughter never sounded like this before. She felt his fingers dig into her side and tickled. Her laughter rang louder. "Cut it out!"

"I love your laugh." He continued to tickle her ribs. "It's beautiful."

She looked up into his expressive brown eyes. Like looking at the dark rich earth lanced with gold and jade. They captivated her. Her laughter died away as she found herself falling deeper and deeper into his gaze. Hypnotic in a way.

His eyes darkened as he looked at her. The heat of his hand warmed her cheek. Her heart swelled with joy. Like a dream, she was the fairy princess and he was her little boy toy. Tonight she would get lucky and enjoy it.

Their lips met. Their tongues touched. Their mouths did a dance as old as time. Her body tightened, felt antsy, like it was going through withdrawals. Withdrawals from something she never really had, but she knew she had to have it soon. The gauzy gown that hung at her waist had been forgotten by her but not by Derrick. With a little help from Derrick it fluttered down her body to pool at her feet.

"Much better."

The gentle glide of his fingers against her skin sent goose bumps racing up and down her arm. She purred at the pleasure her body felt. Those magnificent fingers skated up her arm and across her collarbone. They slid between the valley of her breasts and glided to the tip of one nipple then the other. Her body shuddered. No one had brought her to so close to ecstasy. Her other lovers were only out for themselves. The pleasure racing through her was new and made her realize what she had been missing up to now.

Her purr turned into a growl, as she needed more. Instinct led her to press her body against his. He urged her to lie down on the bed. Nibbling on her ear, he pressed her into the crisp linens on her bed. Between the sensation of the sheets, his kisses and his hands touching her, she was ready to explode.

The only sound she heard was their breathing in unison. Derrick's was as ragged as hers. The scent of their bodies filled the air.

~ * ~

He had heard stories about her sexual prowess, spoken by several of the men who had been her bed partners, but nothing they told him prepared him for this. She reacted to every little thing. Derrick never had a partner who showed so much emotion and he loved it.

He pressed his lips against her neck, nipping just a little each time as he made his way down her throat. Each time her breath caught and she arched that delicious neck a little more. Her salty taste on his tongue was addictive.

Derrick licked her collarbone, drawing a cat-like moan out of G'Linda. A grin spread across his face. If she liked him licking her neck she would love what else he was planning to do with his tongue.

He continued to trace a path down her body, working his way to her left breast. The hardened pink tip called to him. When his mouth closed around it she arched her back and squealed a little. It brought another smile to his face. As his mouth worked its magic on her breast, his hand skimmed along her stomach to her moist heat.

~ * ~

Glenda felt his hand on her mound. Her body was on fire. Deep-seated frustrations from all other encounters flew away. Tension built, higher, tighter then suddenly it fractured, allowing her to soar through her orgasm. Just as she started back to earth, he kissed her stomach before working his way down. When his mouth closed around her core, she arched up off the bed. Her body tightened again. Her breath hitched. She needed him. "Now."

Derrick brought his lips to hers as he centered himself over her body. She helped glide him home to her core.

A gasp escaped her when he slid home. The delicious friction they created as they moved together sent ripples of desire through her. It started to build again. She could feel her muscles tighten, drawing a moan from him.

Her eyes opened wide. Goodness no one ever told her it was this good. Her heart beat a rapid tempo. One that made her feel like flying. Her breath hitched again as her body felt like it was diving off a cliff. Her toes curled up as the orgasm grabbed a hold of her once more. She squeezed her eyes closed as powerful sensations took control. Colors exploded behind her eyelids. A scream filled the air. Her heart beat hard in her chest. "Wow."

Derrick rested his head in the crook of her neck. His body shook as an aftershock rocked him. He placed a kiss on her neck. "Again?"

"Oh, yeah." Now that she knew how good it could be, she'd always want more.

~ * ~

The next morning Glenda dressed and went into the living room, drawn by the wonderful heady aroma of what she would call coffee. Not knowing what word they used, she kept silent until Derrick spotted her.

"Care to break your fast?"

It took her a few minutes before she realized he meant breakfast. "Sure. What do you have?"

"Fruit, bread, left over stew if you'd like some. I have a hot beverage for you if you prefer."

"Yes to the drink." She liked cream and sugar in her coffee and wondered how difficult it would be to get some if she needed it. Taking the cup, she took a sip, hoping it wouldn't be too bitter. Glenda was amazed at its natural sweetness. "This is wonderful. Thank you."

"It's native to our village." He poured himself a drink as well.

"So what shall we do today?" She leaned a hip against the counter he worked against as he fixed something for them to eat.

"Well, the village would like to meet you, if that suits you. They've never seen a witch before."

"About the witch thing." She felt she should come clean. Especially after the night before.

"I'll not use that phrase in front of them if it displeases you." He stopped and bowed. "But they do wish to meet the woman who will save them."

What could she say to that? She gave him a weak smile. "Of course. Glenda the good witch at your service."

He gave her a quick smile before setting a plate of fruit, cheeses, and breads on the counter. "Great. As soon as we are finished we'll go and I'll introduce you to my people."

She nodded.

It didn't take long before their meal was finished and they were headed down to the village. Glenda didn't know what to expect so she was nervous. When they came into view of the first group of houses, she felt butterflies take off at the number of people waiting for them. "Derrick?"

"They are in awe of you. Everyone has come out to meet you." He touched her arm. His way of asking her not to bolt like a frightened animal.

She took a deep breath. It was okay; she could do this. As long as they didn't charge her. Everyone stood in a cluster. They seemed to be more afraid of her than she was of them.

Someone broke out of the crowd. Not very big but moved a lot faster than Glenda could. She was knocked to the ground before she could get out of the way.

"D'Asha, stop." An older woman stepped out of the crowd. The moment she noticed G'Linda she dropped to her knees. "Forgive me. She is just a child."

Glenda nodded as she was helped to her feet. "Her name is Dasha?"

"Yes." Derrick spoke softly. "She is but five."

Glenda grinned. She walked over and helped the woman to her feet. "What is she chasing?"

"Your gift."

"Really?" She looked at Derrick. "I think I'd like to help her."

"But..." He looked uncomfortable.

"No." She shook her head. "Please let me." Glenda took off before he could say anything else. A gift from such a small thing held a world of promise. Something the other Glenda might not like but she was sure she would enjoy.

She dashed down the path Dasha raced down. A flash of yellow caught her eyes. Wasn't that the same color the little girl wore? The

83

sound of a very young voice let her know she was heading in the right direction. "Dasha?"

"Oh, please come back." D'Asha grabbed a slow hanging branch and pulled herself up. "You are ruining everything."

"What is ruining everything?" Glenda asked.

"Oh!" The child turned quickly to see who spoke to her. Her precarious balance shifted and she started to slide off the branch.

Glenda grabbed her before she could hit the ground. "Didn't mean to startle you but your mom told me you had a gift for me."

"I do, but it ran away." Her head dropped in disappointment. "It was to be the best present you could receive."

"And it will be." She set Dasha on her feet. "Let's go look for this gift."

"Oh, we can't find it unless it wants to be found."

Well that was cryptic enough. What did this child create that they had to wait for it to come back at its earliest convenience? "Can you tell me what it is?"

"A kitty."

Now the situation made more sense. The kitten probably was frightened and hiding somewhere. "Does it have a name?"

"Oh, no, I didn't name the kitty. That is your job." Dasha squatted down and peered into the brush. "Maybe if you call her softly she might come out."

"Okay. Tell me about the kitten. What color is her fur?"

"Orange and white striped." The little girl turned to face her. "Very sweet too. She never acted up until now."

"Perhaps she is just a little nervous." Glenda crouched down beside Dasha. "If she was yours to keep, what would you name it?"

"Lightning."

"Really? Why?"

"Because she is so fast, and she has a lightning bolt across her forehead." She showed the shape and location of the mark on her forehead.

"Lightning it is." Glenda looked around. Wherever this kitten was she couldn't find it. A slight movement caught her eye. Just a foot or two in front of her sat the cutest little kitten she ever had seen. She crouched down in front of the feline. "Hello, Lightning."

The cat tilted her head. After a moment or two she stood up and started to trot away.

"Wait!" Glenda took a couple steps forward. "I'm not going to hurt you."

Lightning turned back to look at her for a moment before vanishing from sight.

Chapter Four

"Dasha? That cat just turned invisible!" Glenda was floored at what she saw. The cat just vanished. Cats don't do that.

"My name is D-Asha, not Dasha. Why do you blend the letters together the way you do?" D'Asha stood close and looked up at her. When she didn't answer right away the little girl tugged on her sleeve. "G'Linda?"

"Oh that makes so much more sense! So Derrick is actually D'Eric? Why didn't he correct me?" She slapped her head. "I'm the great and powerful…witch."

D'Asha stepped back in fear.

"I'm sorry." Glenda smiled at her, hoping to waylay her fear. "What does the D stand for?"

"It tells everyone what village you are from." The little girl straightened her shoulders, showing she wasn't afraid of the great witch. It made Glenda smile. "I am from here so a D is put in front of my name and you are from a village where everyone uses a G."

"Um, actually…" What was she going to tell the girl? The truth wouldn't make sense to a child. "I have decided to blend my name since I travel so much. That way it won't seem like I am partial to one village."

"That is very nice of you." D'Asha smiled. "You are not like the stories I was told."

"Thank you." She smiled again and patted the little girl on the head. "I probably surprise everyone, but I promise I'm friendly and hope I can help."

"You'll be my friend?"

"Of course." Glenda knew she needed all the friends she could get, even if they came in munchkin form. She felt something tugging on her dress from the back. Turning, she tried to see what was causing the sensation, but she found nothing. She felt several more tugs. "What is going on?"

"I believe Lightning has decided she likes you. She always sits on my shoulder when she wants to rest."

Glenda stopped moving and felt the slight tug again before something climbed up her back. She heard the purr in her ears just before the slight weight settled in. It brought a smile to her lips. "She has a nice purr, doesn't she?"

D'Asha nodded as she took her hand and led her back to the center of the village. D'Eric's whole body jumped when he spotted her. "G'Linda I was so worried for you! Where have you been?"

"D'Asha and I were looking for my present." She pointed to her shoulder as she turned her head. Nothing was visible. Great, now they were all going to think she was nuts.

"We found Lightning." D'Asha threw her shoulders back to show her pride in their accomplishment. "Did you know the cat could be invisible? She's sitting on Glenda's shoulder right now."

Everyone chuckled. So, invisible cats weren't common things here either. She wouldn't believe it either if it weren't sitting on her shoulder at the moment. She brushed her hands against a set of invisible paws and crouched down beside D'Asha. "Thank you so much for my wonderful gift. I will treasure it always."

"You're welcome." D'Asha bowed her head. "Can I come to visit from time to time?"

"I'll work it out with your mom. Okay?"

She nodded.

D'Eric stood beside her and spoke to the people, making sure they knew who she was. Glenda smiled and nodded at the appropriate times but all the while, she wondered about Lightning. She could feel its weight on her shoulder, hear it purring in her ear, yet no one believed the cat existed.

It is a little strange.

87

The thought floated into her head and she had to agree. It was strange. An invisible cat was right out of a science fiction book.

That doesn't mean I don't exist.

Okay, that was strange. Her thoughts were putting the cat in the first person.

Why do you keep thinking these are your thoughts? I am quite capable of thought.

"G'Linda?"

Confusion filled her. What had she missed? "Yes?"

"D'Erin wants to know if you would like to walk through her fields. Her crops aren't doing that well and she hoped you could do a little magic for her." D'Asha informed her.

Magic? How would she be able to help them and not reveal she was a fake? "I don't know." She felt Lightning's claws biting into her shoulder. "But I'll do my best to see what is wrong."

D'Eric smiled. He gestured to D'Erin to lead the way to her fields.

Glenda spent the whole time trying to figure out how she was going to pull this off. She had no magical power. Being so deep in thought, she wasn't paying attention and ran into the back of D'Eric when he stopped and she didn't. He hit the ground with a grunt. "I'm so sorry, D'Eric. I was focusing my thoughts."

"I understand you must focus to help." He got up and dusted himself off. "I'm fine."

"My crops started growing properly but a couple of weeks ago they started to lose their color. Now they look droopy and sad." D'Erin walked up and touched a couple plants. "Can you help me?"

Glenda walked among the crops, touching one then another. They looked dried and withered. Like they needed water. She looked up at the clear blue sky. "When was the last time it rained around here?"

"It has been a while. Maybe a cycle?" The woman looked at her. "Can you make it rain?"

"I don't want to go through such drastic measures." She bluffed. "But there are things you can do to protect your crops when the rain won't come. Are you near a body of water?"

"Yes. There is a lake close."

"Close enough to build a trench from the lake to your crops? To water them?" It might not work but it would be worth a try. "If we got enough people together maybe we could bring the water to your crops."

"We tried that but the buckets leaked, and by the time we got them to the plants there was no water left."

"Then you don't use any tree sap to seal the holes?" She looked at D'Eric.

"No one has thought of that." He gave her an amazed look. "Your magic runs very deep."

But it wasn't magic; it was just common sense to her. If only she could remember the proper way to build an aqueduct; then again she was lucky she remembered her ancient history enough to think of the sap. "If we made these changes can we get people from the village to come help?"

"Yes. Many are farmers and have the same problem. If we can do it for one, we can do it for all."

"Then let's get started."

~ * ~

That evening they celebrated. Glenda's idea worked and now the whole village had a way to get water to their crops. She still felt they needed a better system than hauling buckets during a draught; but she guessed she'd take this one day at a time. If she could find a way home, she'd look up the info on building an aqueduct.

Someone handed her a drink. While her thoughts continued to flow, she realized she hadn't thought about home in a while. She should be working on getting back to her own world, not fixing this one.

"Are you all right?"

"I'm fine." She was so deep in thought she came close to jumping out of her skin when he spoke to her. Instead, she took a sip of her drink and tried to act natural. "Why?"

"You've been quiet. This party is for you, but you have been hiding over here for over an hour."

"Sorry, but I have a lot on my mind." She gave him her best smile. "From this point on I promise to be the life of the party."

"Excuse me?" He gave her another confused look.

"Never mind. It's a local phrase where I'm from. It means I promise to have a good time."

"Life of the party. Has a nice ring to it." He draped an arm over her shoulder. "Come."

She smiled and allowed him to lead her to the small cluster of people. She loved the heat of his body so close to hers. It made her feel protected when she found the people of the village standing around watching her. No one spoke. Oh yeah, this was fun. Being stared at like she was some exotic animal in the zoo was something she really enjoyed. Moments ticked by. "Somebody say something."

Three started talking at once. None of them made any sense but at least the silence was broken. Everyone started to talk then. They asked her a million questions, ones she couldn't answer so she winged it.

"How long have you been a witch?"

That was a good question. "All my life? I've been using my powers as long as I can remember." She didn't know if it was true but it seemed to appease everyone. They all smiled and nodded.

"Can you tell us a story about how you saved another village?"

"Most of my stories precede me so I'm sure you've heard them before." She smiled at them, hoping this would keep them from asking more questions. "I don't think I can tell them any better than what you've already heard."

They nodded and murmured.

Good. It looked like they would accept her answer. "How is D'Asha? I haven't seen her this evening."

"She is feeling under the weather so her mother kept her home," said one of the ladies. "She does wish she was here and hopes you're enjoying her gift."

"Very much." Glenda petted the invisible front paws of Lightning, who sat perched on her shoulder. Too bad no one here believed the cat was real.

"It's time for us to go home," D'Eric spoke softly in her ear. His voice sent shivers down her spine. It made her very aware of him.

The sun was setting and most of the people were preparing to go home, but hadn't left. They were waiting for her to make the first move.

She nodded and turned to the people. "Thank you for this wonderful celebration. I'll see you in the morning."

D'Eric slipped a hand into the small of her back and steered her toward the house. All she could think about was they were going back to the house alone with lots of time on their hands. The thought of the night's events had her blood rushing through her veins.

The village lined up behind them. Hurrying home before the sun set.

They did the same thing. Racing time.

They stepped into the house just as the sun dipped behind the horizon. "We should make it a practice to come inside before the sun sets."

"Hey, this time wasn't my fault." She smiled as she sat in one of two chairs now surrounding the table. Her thoughts dwelled on all the things they could do to each other this evening, but she wasn't going to let him know what she was thinking. "You guys wanted to have a party."

"True, but you don't fear the night and could make me forget what is out there to hurt the people in the village." He puttered about in the kitchen, coming out with two drinks for them. He placed them on the table and sat. "Why don't you fear what is out there?"

"There are always dangerous things in the night but you can't let them control you with fear." She picked up the cup he placed on the table and rolled it in the palm of her hands. It helped keep her mind off how his body moved. She knew what was under the robe and it had her heart beating harder. "I know what I'm capable of and I trust myself."

"True." He sat in the other chair. "But you are a witch. You can protect yourself."

That wasn't what she meant, but D'Eric wouldn't understand even if she tried to explain. "I try not to rely on my powers, but on my mind and my abilities. I tend to rely on myself."

"Have you had problems with your powers?"

That might work. She was amazed she could keep track of the conversation. Her eye candy was very distracting. "Yes."

He sat back in the chair. "That must be frightening. I can't imagine having all that power and not being able to use it."

"Which is why I've learned to rely on me instead of my powers." She sure hoped he didn't figure out she was lying. Heat filled her cheeks. Was it from her wandering thoughts, or the fear he'd learn the truth? "I only use my powers in extreme cases. The rest of the time I'm trying to solve matters on my own."

"That is very noble."

"Power used frivolously can corrupt." Glenda took a sip from her cup. Her drink had a nice fruity taste. She wondered what he'd do if she poured it all over him then licked it off. The heat in her cheeks deepened. Why he brought these types of thoughts she didn't know. It never happened before. "What is this? It's very good."

"It's one of our evening drinks." He gave her a bone melting smile and a silent toast. "Helps relax you, and makes you giggle if you drink too much."

"Ah. We have something like that at home." She took a sip. "But it has a tendency to make some people downright stupid or obnoxious." It also had a tendency to lower inhibitions and raises your libido.

"I have heard of drinks like that. We are lucky the medicinal berries we use don't affect the body that way. Then again I don't think we would use them if they had any negative effect."

"You'd be surprised what people will drink to alter their reality." She took another sip. "So what have you planned for the evening?"

"I thought you might enjoy a bath this evening. I've already brought the tub in, all I need to do is heat the water for you, add a few oils, and you can relax and soothe your muscles."

It went right along with her wayward thoughts. Perfect. "I'd like that."

"Good." He smiled and stood. "I'll get the water ready."

Within fifteen minutes, he had hot water and was pouring it into the large wooden tub setting in the middle of the floor. "The oils are on the dresser. Why don't you pick one to use?"

She shrugged and walked over to the dresser covered with a bunch of little bottles. Lifting the small stoppers, she sniffed one bottle after another, wondering if she would find the right scent. She only liked the very soft scents, nothing overpowering. Most of the bottles were concentrated fragrances that made her nose curl and her eyes water.

"Not finding anything you like?"

"Sorry, but they're all a bit strong." She set one of the bottles she had in her hand on the dresser.

"I have one other, but most of the people in the village felt it had no scent. Maybe it would be what you'd like." He stepped out of the room for a moment and returned with another small bottle. "How about this?"

She took the bottle with a smile. Lifting the snifter, she took a whiff. "Oh, I like this."

"Then everything is ready. Those buckets over there have cold water to get the temperature where you want it." He stepped to the door. "There is a large cloth on the bed you can use to dry yourself when you're done. I'll be in the kitchen cleaning up. Call me if you need any help."

She gave him a sultry look. "Help, huh? Want to scrub my back?"

"All in good time." He gave her a sensual smile of his own. "You enjoy the bath first."

Glenda sighed as he closed the door. She poured in a little of the oil before adding some of the colder water. Once she had the temperature just right she brought the bath sheet closer to the tub and started to remove her clothes. One shoulder was a little hard to undress because of the cat. "This would be so mush easier if you would climb off and amuse yourself elsewhere long enough for me to bathe."

She felt the rough brush of a tongue before the cat jumped onto the bed. "What about becoming visible? I'll forget what you look like if I don't see you enough."

Two little paws showed first before the cat showed totally. Predominantly black, the cat had a white chest with four white paws and a zigzag of the same color over its brow. It walked around in a circle for a few moments before settling against the comforter. Lightning curled up in a small ball as she watched Glenda prepare for her bath.

Glenda came over and ruffled the cat's fur. "You sure are cute. Too bad no one can see you or they'd agree with me."

The cat tilted its head at her.

"I almost believe you can understand me." She grinned and petted the cat once more. Just as she stepped into the water, she realized she still wore the crystal necklace her grandmother gave her. The satin string that held it could get damaged in the water. "Oops, almost forgot about you." Glenda pulled the necklace off.

"No!" screamed the cat as it leaped back onto her shoulder, just before she disappeared from the room.

Glenda found herself standing stark naked in a dressing room of some department store.

Chapter Five

"Holy cow!" The door to the little booth stood ajar. She peeked around and found herself in a darkened department store. Seconds later she slammed it shut. "How the heck did I get back here?"

"You took the necklace off."

Glenda looked around. The room was dark but someone could have been hiding in here. Did she land in a dressing room that was already occupied? "Who's talking?"

"Me."

She shook her head. "And who is me?"

Something sighed.

Lightning leaped off her shoulder again and materialized as it hit the small cushioned chair in the counter. "It was me."

Glenda stared at the cat. "You've got to be kidding. There's no such thing as a talking cat. Except in cartoons."

"Okay. So pretend I'm animated. We have to go back." Lightning arched her back.

"Right." She crossed her arms over her breasts. "A talking cat from another dimension who knows about cartoons."

"Actually the term another dimension isn't exactly correct but we don't have time to go into that right now." The cat flexed her claws. "We must go back now."

"And how am I supposed to do that?"

"The necklace. It's a teleportation device tuned into a particular plane. Please put it back on."

"Why?"

"One, you're not dressed." The cat sat on the chair, placing her paws in front of her and curling her tail around her body. "Two, your world is not a safe place for something like me. Three, it's after hours here, and this store is closed. You'll be accused of breaking and entering, and let's not forget about indecent exposure."

She crossed to the door and unlocked it. Peeking out, she found Lightning was right. Glenda let out a sigh of relief. She turned back to the cat. "How the heck do you know so much about my world? This is like a science fiction show. Something I'd see on the SciFi channel."

"I promise to explain everything if you will just go back."

"Boy, are you crabby!" Glenda picked up the cat and donned the necklace. In an instant, they were back in the bedroom. "See? All safe and sound."

Lightning leaped out of her arms, stuck her tail up in the air, and walked a wide berth around the tub. She jumped up on the bed and curled into a ball once again.

A knock on the thick wooden door made the thing vibrate. "Are you all right G'Linda?"

She grabbed the big bath sheet and wrapped it around her before opening the door. "I'm fine."

"I thought I heard you talking to someone." D'Eric stepped in and looked around. He passed so close to her she could feel the heat from his body.

"Guess I must have been talking out loud to myself." She looked around and found nothing wrong. Steam still hung over the water in the tub so she knew she hadn't been gone long. Checking the bed, she found Lightning had faded from sight.

"I've been known to do that myself." He gave her a bright smile. "If you'd like, I could wash your back now."

"Can you give me a few minutes?" She smiled back. "This might sound silly but I haven't even gotten the chance to get into the water and soak a little. I'd like to be able to do that. How about I call you when I'm ready?"

He wiggled his eyebrows at her and pulled the door closed behind him when he left the room.

Glenda dropped the cloth and stepped into the water. A groan escaped her as the heat seeped into her bones. "So?"

What?

Great, now I'm supposed to believe Lightning can speak to me mentally. She dropped her head against the back of the tub.

I can hear your thoughts as well. You'll find it very helpful when you need info and can't ask any questions.

You honestly expect me to believe that a normal cat can became invisible and talk? Glenda sunk into the water a little more.

Who says humans are the only ones who can talk? Perhaps you are the only ones who can't use telepathy to speak to each other.

Okay, okay. I'm sorry. You're right I'm being an idiot. I shouldn't judge. She opened one eye and looked at the bed. *So why did you make me come back here?*

We weren't ready to go to your world. You and I have a lot to talk about. If you go home, you must promise to come back.

Why? She sat up in the tub. *This isn't my world. I don't belong here.*

Because these people need you here.

They need the real G'Linda. She has the power to subdue whatever is out there. I'm just a journalist with far too much time on my hands. I can't fix these people's problems.

There is a reason you're here. That necklace wouldn't have activated if you weren't needed to help these people. The witch can't fix their problem. You can.

Now that's crazy talk.

You aren't ready to talk about this. We'll finish this conversation in the morning after you've had time to think about it.

Glenda sunk back in the tub and sighed. This was crazy. She couldn't be this little village's savior.

She heard another knock and smiled. Her back rub was back. "Come in."

The door opened slowly. "I was waiting for you to call me back in."

"Sorry. Guess I got lost in thought. Come on in." She watched D'Eric step into the room and close the door behind him. Her body tingled at the thought of his hands on her.

"And what had you so deep in thought?" He crossed to the dresser and picked a small bottle sitting toward the back.

"My gift from D'Erin and your problem." At least she wasn't lying. She had been thinking about what the cat had said to her. Glenda still didn't believe her but it did have her thinking. "That creature hasn't been around tonight."

"It shows up every night, sometimes early, sometimes late." He poured a liquid in his hands and rubbed them together. "Do you mind if I ask you a question? You've changed your accent since you've been here. Why?"

"Accent?" She didn't get what he was talking about.

"The way you say our names. You said them differently before." He continued to rub his hands together to heat up the oil to body temperature.

"Ah. D'Erin explained how you say your names. I didn't realize that the first letter was said separately. Where I come from we blend it together. Like my name. I'm used to hearing Glenda, all one word. Not G'Linda."

"I will try to say it your way." He held up his hands once the oil was heated to his liking.

"You don't have to. I've gotten use to the way you say it and I kind of like it. It's endearing." She gave him a soft smile.

He smiled back. Stepping up to the tub, he knelt behind her. His hands touched her shoulders, pausing for a moment before starting the massage.

Heat seeped into her bones as his hands worked on her back. Strong fingers kneaded tight muscles. A sigh escaped her as she dropped her head forward. "That feels so good."

"I'm glad you approve." His voice whispered softly in her ears. It sent goose bumps racing up her arms. "I have been told I give the best massages."

"You've been told? Just how many of your talents have been voted number one?" The thought that he shared his gifts so easily made her wonder just what he did before she showed up here.

"It's not important." He dipped his hands into the water and splayed them on the small of her back. Using delicious pressure, he eased muscles she didn't know where so tight.

"Wow." Her head lolled a little on her shoulders. If he kept this up, she'd slip spineless to the bottom of the tub.

He continued to work on her back until she was a wet noodle. Warm, strong hands slipped under her and pulled her to her feet. She felt the bath sheet surround her before she became weightless. "Are you carrying me?"

"You seem very relaxed and I didn't want to make you walk all the way to the bed." He set her on the soft comforter. "I didn't want you to tense up on me so I thought this would be so much better."

"I could fall asleep right now." Her voice came out as a whisper, like she didn't have the muscles to speak.

"No, no. I have other plans for you this evening. If you fall asleep on me I just might have to tickle you to keep you awake." He gave her a wicked smile. "Although I do have other ways to keep you alert."

"Really? Like what?" She arched her brow at him. What did he have in mind? The thought sent tingles to her toes.

"Would you like me to show you what I do to people who fall asleep on me?"

"Shall I pretend to be asleep to make it more realistic?" She wiggled her eyebrows at him. "I can play the part if you need me to."

"Willing is always good." He climbed on the bed with her.

Then he sat there with a strange look on his face. Why was he just sitting there? "Is there a problem?"

"What? Oh, no. I was just enjoying the view. You are so beautiful."

She felt the blush his words brought flush her body from head to toe. Instinct had her reaching for the cover to hide her body.

"No. Please don't." He grabbed the comforter and pulled it back. "You have a beautiful body, so sexy and passion filled. Last night filled me with such joy. I've never been with a woman who showed so much passion."

How should she take this? No one ever said things like that to her. It embarrassed her and thrilled her. This was a man she could spend the rest of her life with, if he would have her. Yet she should know better. From the stories he had told her he might be the town gigolo and wouldn't want to give up that job. Not a good path for her mind to follow so she shook herself mentally.

D'Eric didn't give her time to think about much else. He leaned in to capture her lips with his. The pressure he used was just enough to melt her a little more. She opened her mouth to allow his tongue entrance. Tingles raced up and down her spine as their tongues entwined. Intense pure joy shot through her.

His hands were busy too. They caressed her breasts, stroked her legs. His lips pressed against the soft tissue of her throat. Nipping along the way. A whimper must have escaped her because he paused. "You okay?"

"Oh, yes. It just feels so good."

"Good, because I've just started." His lips merged with hers again as he reached under the bed. He wiggled a little as he tried to find something.

"Problem?" Her voice came out deep and throaty.

"Looking for something. Give me a second." He slid his upper body over the edge of the bed as he plopped his palms on the floor. His butt wiggled and bunched as he moved along the floor. "There you are you little devil. Come here."

"D'Eric?" She kept watching his butt move and thought about giving it a pinch. The only reason she didn't was because she feared he'd whack his head on the bed frame in shock.

He came back up with a grin and a huge feather. "Thought I'd try a little sensory pleasure."

She gave him an arched brow. "Getting a little playful? Can I use it on you too?"

"Of course. I was hoping you would." He slid the feather across her stomach and heard her breath suck in. "But you are first."

His impish grin made her heart flutter. The feather swished around her stomach one more time, forcing her to lie flat on the bed. It wasn't going to take much to put her over the edge tonight.

The feather slid around her hip and fluttered down one leg before gliding up the other. D'Eric took his time moving the feather, flicking and circling some of his favorite parts of her body. A nipple, the inside of her thigh, the juncture of her legs, against her collarbone. Each swirl inched her closer to the brink of her release. She could feel her body sing with every brush. Glenda wasn't sure if she could take much more. "D'Eric, please."

"You have such a beautiful body, I love watching your body react to my ministrations." He flicked the feather against a nipple, making her body arch. "The passion you show is awing and arousing." Seconds later, he swirled his tongue against the same nipple.

A groan escaped her. "Now, D'Eric. I can't take much more."

He slid his body across hers. "There is much more pleasure I can give you with the feather."

"I know that, but my body doesn't want the feather now. It wants you. Now. Deep inside me before I explode."

He poised himself just outside her before slamming into her. A scream of joy ripped from her throat as she felt him penetrate her body. Her muscles tightened against him, enjoying the delicious slide of his hardened member. Tingles of joy zinged through her blood.

She pumped her hips against him, forcing a quickened pace. It felt too good. Her body tightened more, like a vice against him. Her orgasm was close. She could feel the beginnings of the freefall she had felt last night. Glenda quickened the pace again.

A keening sound escaped her as they drew closer and closer to their release. An intense pressure built up inside her, building and building until she felt her body soar. She flew above the clouds, feeling the wind in her hair against her skin. Joy filled her as she dipped and dived across an imaginary sky.

Moments later she felt D'Eric tighten before he reached his pinnacle as well. He relaxed against her.

"It's my turn with the feather." She gave him an impish smile.

Chapter Six

The next morning she sat in her chair, grasping the steaming cup in her hands. Last night had been wonderful. The feather had come into play several times through the night, giving them both a lot of pleasure.

She felt the weight on her shoulder lift as a soft thump vibrated against the table.

We need to talk.

D'Eric worked in the kitchen, preparing breakfast. Glenda looked at him for a moment before looking at the empty table. *Now? He's still here.*

And he always will be. He can't hear our conversation unless you start talking out loud instead of using your mind.

The little fur ball was being a tad obnoxious. *Speaking mentally isn't something I'm used to, but you don't have to rub it in.*

I thought you'd like to visit your home.

I know I can do that. All I have to do is take this necklace off. She gestured toward the crystal to emphasize her words.

Don't! I'd like to make sure you understand all the rules before we head to your world.

What rules?

The cat sat up a little more. *Nothing you can't handle, but the best way to do this is for you to understand that I should go with you. And if I do you're obligated to come back here so I can return to my home.*

I don't need you.

Actually, you do. There are things you don't know about your world that I must explain. I need to show you where the gates are to my world.

There are several places where it is easy to cross over.

You mean, others have come here?

Yes. Lightning licked a paw then rubbed it against her head. *We've had many visitors over the years. I even remember your grandmother.*

How? You're a kitten. You were born, what maybe six weeks ago?

And you know I'm not a normal cat either. Lightning continued to clean herself by licking her paw and applying it to areas she couldn't reach with her tongue.

You saying you're over fifty years old? Glenda couldn't believe this, but Lightning was right. She had a lot of talents no other cat had.

Thank you for the compliment but I'm more than three hundred years old.

No way.

It's true. Now she started washing her back. *I am the only one of my kind.*

And what if something happened to you? Glenda hadn't known the cat for long but she already felt a bond to it. Its uniqueness made the creature very special.

Don't worry about me. Nothing has happened to me in three hundred years, I doubt anything will.

We're pretty sure of ourselves aren't we?

As time goes on you'll understand why I seem this way. Lightning lifted one leg and proceeded to clean it. *But I want to get back to what we were talking about.*

Okay, let's say I take you with me to my world. How do we go without D'Eric realizing that I've disappeared? The boy doesn't let me out of his sight.

Leave that to me. The cat winked at her.

How do I prepare for this?

There is nothing you need to do other than follow my lead.

Glenda nodded. D'Eric came back into the room, pulling his chair out so he could sit and enjoy his cup too. "Breakfast will be ready in a minute or two."

"Thanks." Glenda took a sip of her neglected drink. "Um, what do you have planned for today?"

"Not much. This is our normal day of rest." He sat his coffee down.

Barbara Donlon Bradley

"There are a few people who have invited you to their homes, but I haven't figured out how to visit each of them without showing favor."

"Why not use the meeting hall again?"

"Why?" He gave her a confused look.

"Invite all the people who want me to visit to the meeting hall and have each of them bring their favorite dishes. That way they won't feel like one family is better than another and I can see all of them."

"And what about the people who might want to come once they learn about us having a gathering there?"

"We could do the same thing tomorrow then." She took a sip. "I don't want to hurt anyone's feelings."

"You are wise." He got up and walked to the small kitchen. "The people will be very happy with your idea."

"I'm just using common sense." She watched him serve their food and walk back to the table. "I'd like to do a ritual today. Is there time for me to do that?"

"Of course." He sat their plates on the table before placing his hands on the back of his chair. "I would be honored to assist you."

"Thank you, D'Eric, I truly appreciate it, but this is something I must do myself." Glenda swallowed, hoping he understood she needed to be alone and it had nothing to do with him.

He smiled and nodded. "I hoped I could watch but I have been told you like your privacy for these things. When do you want to proceed?"

"After breakfast?"

He jumped up.

"Finish your meal." She lifted her cup. "Besides, I might want a little more of this before I head off."

~ * ~

Glenda stood near the clearing where she first appeared in this foreign land. *Okay, this is it. Taking off my necklace.* Lightning's answering silence made her shrug. She could feel the weight of the cat but didn't understand why it hadn't answered. Grasping the crystal by the chain, she lifted it over her head and watched the world spin around her once again. She found herself back in the bathroom of the restaurant.

Now, understand no time has passed here in your world.

You mean, I'm still on my date? She couldn't believe it. *What about the department store?*

We arrived there because you were in a different location. Your date thought you were still in the bathroom. Time doesn't pass in your world when you're not here. It's one of the reasons why I had you put your clothing on under the cloak. I'm not sure how he would accept the change in clothing so fast.

Right. The cloak wouldn't go over real big. Glenda hadn't gotten past the point that she was back home. She pulled the cloak off and folded it up. Walking to the last stall in the bathroom, she stuffed the cloak up behind the tank. Once she was sure no one would find it she walked back out. *So, I'm still on my date? That's just so wrong. He was awful. The most boring man I had ever met.*

Then you have more incentive to get out of here quickly.

Believe me. I already had the incentive before I found a talking invisible cat on my shoulders. You just be careful. He likes to grab at body parts. He doesn't care which one. She took a deep breath before heading out of the bathroom. It took her a moment or two to acclimate to the room again. Where were they sitting?

Oh yeah. The maniac waving at her was her date. Even though no time had passed, he acted like she had been gone too long and feared she had forgotten where they sat. Thank goodness he had no tact. "Brian. Was I gone too long?"

"I was getting a little worried."

She smiled down at him before taking her seat. "Sorry. Needed to fix my makeup a little."

"Not a problem, although if you had asked me you would have known that fixing your makeup was a waste of time."

She batted her eyelashes as she heard Lightning whisper in her mind. *I see what you mean.*

He doesn't understand how people interpret what he says. His double edge comment was one of the reasons I wanted to get out of the date. I think that's why I wished to be out of here.

Is that how you ended up in my world? Because you wanted to get away from this bozo?

Pretty much.

Wonderful. So you have no idea what your destiny is. The cat adjusted herself on Glenda's shoulder. *First things first. We need to get out of here.*

Destiny?

I'll explain later. Focus on the goal at hand.

The waiter had just brought their meal when she sat down. She had planned on dashing out the door, but the food smelled delicious and her stomach picked that particular moment to growl loudly.

"Guess you're hungry. Dig in." Brian speared a piece of his steak and shoved it into his mouth.

Being hungry, she decided to eat and chose to ignore Lightning, who sunk her claws into Glenda's shoulder when she didn't jump up from the table as fast as the cat wanted. *I'm hungry, so you'll have to wait.*

Lightning didn't say anything but Glenda could feel the dissatisfaction of the little cat. The meal was delicious and she planned on enjoying every bite. "Brian, you picked a great restaurant."

"I've always loved the food here." He shoveled a forkful into his mouth, but that didn't stop him from continuing to talk. "Try to come here about once a week."

She ducked her head so she wouldn't have to see any food falling out of his mouth as he spoke. In her time away, she had forgotten how disgusting he was. It made her shiver. Just how fast could she finish her meal?

Claws dug deeper into her shoulder. She felt like she was wolfing her food down but she couldn't help it. Getting out of here without Brian was her number one priority. After she put her last bite in her mouth, she stood up. "Brian, thanks so much, unfortunately I got a call from a friend of mine while I was in the bathroom and there's been an emergency. I have to go."

"But…" he stood up, but Glenda was already heading to the door.

Once she bolted out the door, and made fast tracks between her and the restaurant, she stopped rushing and took a breath. "Happy?" The soft purr in her ear said yes.

She walked the long distance to her apartment. With an invisible cat on her shoulder, she felt it was safe. "As long as we don't get mugged."

"Don't worry. We won't." Lightning settled into the soft gate she

106

set. "Your city is very strange."

"Have you never been here?" They spoke in soft tones, but she knew a woman talking to herself while walking the streets at night normally meant crazy, thus ensuring people would give her a wide berth.

"About a hundred years ago. One of the reasons I wanted to come here was I had heard so much about this place and wanted to see how much it has changed. From what I see, it's changed a lot."

"Some of the sights might still be familiar, but it depends on where you went the last time." It took them about a half an hour to reach her apartment. Once they were inside and the door was locked, she plopped on the couch. "Now why did we come back here? Just for you to sightsee? I could have come home and stayed if it weren't for you."

"I know and that's the one thing you can't do right now. My world needs you." Lightning jumped to the coffee table in front of the couch. "You came to our world on purpose, whether you believe it or not. G'linda won't help these people when she arrives."

"You mean, she's coming?"

"Yes, and you must send her away."

"And what if I don't want to?"

Chapter Seven

Glenda didn't want to be drawn into the problems of people she barely knew. She had enough of her own. "Why me?"

"Why not you?" Lightning dropped to the floor and started to look around the apartment.

"Where the heck are you going?" Glenda was hot on her heels. "We need to talk."

"You didn't want to talk a few minutes ago when I said the same thing." She nosed the door to the bathroom open and wandered in.

"That was different." Glenda walked into the bathroom and shooed her back out. "You need to explain that doom and gloom comment."

"Was that a toilet? What do your cats use?"

"A litter box. Now get back on the subject."

"G'Linda needs to be sent away from the village when she shows up, and you're the one who must banish her from the area. There are a few things here you can use to prove you have stronger powers than she does."

"I'm not a witch." She wandered into the kitchen. Opening the refrigerator, she pulled out a can of soda and a carton of milk. Once she got a small bowl from the cabinet, she filled it with milk and set it on the floor. "How am I supposed to defeat one who is?"

"G'Linda isn't a witch anymore than you are. She preys on small towns to gain wealth. If a true witch were to show up she would learn her lesson and leave everyone alone." Lightning paused in front of the bowl and took a sniff. "What is that?"

"Milk. I thought you might be thirsty."

She wrinkled her nose at it. "Sure doesn't smell like milk."

"Just drink it, or don't. I don't really care." Glenda walked back into the living room. "I think it's time for you to go back."

"I haven't convinced you, have I?" Lightning trotted in behind her.

"No."

"Okay. Then at least let me show you the doors to my world." She sat at Glenda's feet with her tail wrapped around her feet.

"How can I say no when you look so cute?"

~ * ~

The hum of the computer filled the room.

"You can see your town from here?" Lightning was amazed.

"I can see the whole world from here. I thought this would be the easiest way to mark the location of your portals. Then I can keep the information in my computer for the future."

"Okay." The cat tilted her head. "So how does it work?"

"You tell me where the doors are and I'll pinpoint them on this map. We know that one is in the bathroom of the restaurant." Glenda placed a small star on the map she had copied from a website.

"Another is one mile due east. The third is one mile due south and one mile due west." Lightning perched on her shoulder once again, watched Glenda make the different marks.

"Then it's a box."

"Yes. These doors are for my village. There are more through your country, but they lead to other villages."

"So your world is built on top of mine?"

"It's hard to explain. We exist between time and space. You can spend years in my world and no time will pass here, but when you spend time here time passes quickly in my world."

"This corner is my building. There's been a doorway all this time and I didn't know it?" She pulled the necklace out of her pocket and sat it on the desk.

"Just remember gravity."

"Excuse me?"

"How many stories up are we right now?"

"About three."

"That's how far up from the ground you'll be if you were to put the necklace on right now."

"Make sure I'm on the bottom floor. Got it." She sat back in her chair. "Can anyone cross the threshold, or must you have a crystal?"

"It is said those with the purest of hearts can come to my world but the only visitors we've ever had always brought the crystal." Lightning shifted her weight. "There are a few things we need to pick up before we head back."

"Unless we can buy them at Wal-Mart, it will have to wait until morning."

"We need baking soda, a prism, and matches."

"Those are some odd items, but we might be in luck."

~ * ~

About an hour later, they stood in the bathroom of the restaurant. "Here we go."

Glenda wrapped the cape around her shoulders once again, careful not to smother Lightning, and donned the crystal. She felt the same weird sensations she had before. Once they passed she found herself back in the wooded area. "So where does the door in my building lead?"

To the clearing behind the house."

"Wow, that's convenient." They walked through the village and back to the house.

D'Eric ran out of the house the moment he saw her. "There you are. You have been gone so long."

"How long?" She didn't like the concern on his face.

"It doesn't matter," said a new voice. "I'm here now."

She saw the woman walking toward them. "And you must be G'Linda."

A confused look crossed the woman's face, as well as D'Eric's. Then she spoke. "I hear you have been impersonating me."

The witch must have expected her to lie, and D'Eric couldn't understand why he had two witches on his hands. "I never said my name was G'Linda, it's Gl-en-da. You guys just assumed I was the same person."

"But you said you were the witch, G'Linda."

110

"Nope." She shook her head. She hated lying, but Lightning kept whispering words in her ear that flew out of her mouth before she could stop them. "If you remember I mumbled something about being Glenda, the good witch of the north. Not this imposter."

Ha!" G'Linda threw her head back and laughed. "I'm not the imposter."

"These people asked for your help. What took you so long to get here?" Glenda placed her hands on her hips. "I came right away."

She sputtered a lame response that made Glenda want to laugh. So far, the other woman was not looking good. A small crowd gathered and continued to grow until all the villagers surrounded them.

"I was working with another village and could not leave until I removed their problem." She crossed her arms and gave Glenda a superior look.

"Right, what was their problem? A well blockage? No wait. I bet it was a strange creature stalking their village." She remembered the stories she had heard about herself, and it seemed every village this G'Linda visited had the same problem. Could she be causing the problem just so she could sweep in, save the day, and get a hefty reward in the process?

Glenda felt a soft purr in her ear just before Lightning leaped off her shoulder. What was she up to now?

"What I do for these people is no secret." She opened her arms. "It's my specialty."

"What other magic do you have?" Glenda wanted to hit herself. That question could come back to bite her in the butt.

G'Linda glared at her. "You'll see soon enough. And you?"

"I did ask first. I want to see what kind of power you have. If I think your power is stronger and can help these people better, then I'll step aside." Why was she digging the hole she started deeper? Why couldn't she just keep her mouth shut?

"Fine." G'Linda made a big show of getting herself ready, flapping sleeves and moving her cloak behind her.

Glenda spotted the large crystal hanging about her neck a few seconds before she disappeared. In seconds, she was back in front of them. Everyone gasped. She gave G'Linda a sly smile. She could play this game. She grasped the necklace and whispered a few words, just like she had seen the other woman do. In seconds she stood in her world. "Learned something new."

Whispering again, she stood back in front of the people and got the same amount of gasps. G'Linda didn't look too happy. "You mock me? I know how to fix this." She reached out and grabbed Glenda's necklace, yanking it off her neck.

"Oh crap." She stood back in the basement of her apartment building. Now what was she going to do?

Chapter Eight

"How am I going to get back there?" Glenda was home. She could stay. That wasn't her world anyway. Yet right now, all she could think about was the people in the village who needed her to protect them from that charlatan. She had to focus. There had to be a way.

Tears streamed down her face as she pressed against the walls to no avail. She pounded, pleaded, and ended up propping her head against a wall in misery. Failure was a word she hated so much, but she had to admit she failed. "No." She pushed against the wall she had been leaning on and stood up. "I can't fail. They need me."

Her fingers splayed against the wall. "Lightning told me this was a portal and I don't need the crystal to get there." She closed her eyes and concentrated on D'Eric. His face caught in passion. The compassion she found in his eyes when he spoke to her. Then her thoughts shifted to Lightning. A gift, a pet, and her confidante. She needed the cat.

The wall started to waver. She could feel her hand pass through it. Pure joy shot through her. In moments, she stood back in the clearing she had left only fifteen minutes before. The clearing was empty now, but she could hear a roar in the distance and knew she'd be able to find everyone easily. Her legs pumped as she ran toward the sounds. No one saw her approaching.

Her brow crinkled when she got a good look at the scene. G'Linda stood a few feet in front of the people, wielding her pendant. In front of her, was a large white tiger growling and pacing. The more she watched the more she noticed the cat was limping, favoring one paw.

The sudden presence of extra weight on her right shoulder let her know Lightning had found her.

Where have you been?

Little jerk took my crystal and it took me a little while to activate the doorway.

You need to get in there. G'Linda is not doing well with her pet.

So the creature that has been terrorizing your world is from my world.

They are native to this world but a few have wandered into yours. G'Linda has had her crystal since she was a child and came to this world when she was bored in her own. The cat became her friend when it was a cub.

Glenda walked though a small cluster of villagers who stood watching the day's events with shocked eyes. They whispered and stepped aside when they saw her. She stepped in front of G'Linda and approached the large feline. She felt the now familiar push against her shoulder as Lightning jumped from her shoulder to land in front of the cat.

"My, you're a pretty thing." She used a soft voice as she inched closer. "I want to help you. You have something in your paw and I can get it out." She could hear Lightning purring and meowing as she dropped down in front of the big cat. Glenda sure hoped whatever Lightning was telling it kept it from taking a swipe at her. Those claws could cause a lot of damage.

She dropped to her knees and continued to speak softly to the cat. *Find out what its name is.*

Snowball.

"Snowball." What a perfect name. "I need to see your paw. The one that hurts. I can make the pain go away."

Snowball growled and pulled that paw back.

"You can understand me? Even better. I promise to make the pain go away." She looked into the big cat's eyes, hoping she showed her sincerity.

The big cat unfurled the wounded paw, howling softly when she felt a sharp pain. Glenda could see the sharp bramble caught between the pads. It was like a small vine with several sharp barbs protruding out. No wonder the poor thing was in pain.

"What did you step in?" Glenda could see damage to several pads on this paw, she wondered if they were all cut up like this. She grabbed the vine and with a gentle touch, she eased the vine and the barbs free of the paw. Sweat broke out on her brow while she worked. One wrong move and she'd do more damage. Finally, the whole thing came free and she threw it away. The paw now started to bleed freely.

Place your hand a few inches above the paw. Lightning jumped back up onto Glenda's shoulder.

She held her hand out. *Now what?*

Heal her.

I don't have that ability.

Just do it.

Glenda sighed and closed her eyes. Heat flowed from her shoulder to her hand. She opened one eye and found her hand bathed in a golden glow. The wounds were quickly closing. It didn't take long before the pad shone a healthy color. She heard a loud purr just before she got knocked to the floor.

Snowball was so grateful she climbed on top of Glenda and proceeded to lick her face. Her laughter filled the air. It seemed to break the spell that kept the villagers from moving.

D'Eric came to her side. "Glenda?" Her name didn't roll off the tongue the first time but she knew it would with a little practice. "What shall we do with G'Linda?"

That was a good question. She had caused a lot of mischief. "What do you normally do to someone who is bad?"

"It's never happened before."

Snowball hadn't moved, just now she rested her head in the spot between Glenda's shoulder and neck. She ran her fingers through the thick fur. "What do you think we should do, Snowball? She is your master."

Snowball lifted her head and growled at G'Linda. The woman cringed.

"I see. You're not real happy with her." She pushed at the heavy weight. "I need to take care of this so you're going to have to get off me."

The cat whimpered but moved off, freeing Glenda to rise to her feet.

Glenda turned and faced G'Linda.

"First, you have something of mine and I want it back." She held out her hand. Her crystal felt warm when it rested in her palm once more. "Now since you took advantage of these people you shouldn't be able to come here anymore. Give me your crystal."

"No! This is mine." She clutched it.

Touch the stone.

Glenda shrugged and did what she was told. She heard Lightning mumble in her ear. The stone glowed brightly.

"What are you do…?" And G'Linda was gone.

Where did she go?

Back to your world.

And when were you going to tell me you had magical powers?

Knew you'd figure it out sooner or later.

Anything else I should be aware of?

Might be a few things, but we can talk about that later.

D'Eric hovered nearby.

"Please relax."

"But I doubted you. I left when you disappeared that last time." He bowed deep in front of her.

"I wasn't sure what was going to happen either. We both doubted me." She entwined her fingers with his.

"I should be punished." He sounded so dejected.

"All right."

"What?" He stared at her wide eyed and swallowed hard.

"Yep. And I know the perfect punishment. You are to be my slave in my bed for a long, long time." She gave him a wink and a smile.

"I think I'm going to like this punishment."

"I promise you will." She called Snowball to her side and they all headed back to the cabin.

She never thought she'd live up to her name, but with a crystal and an invisible cat she learned anything was possible. With a wink and a smile she said, "Time to start your punishment."

THE END

Picture Perfect

Picture Perfect

Susan sat with her girlfriends at the local coffee shop. She loved her friends but she wished they would stop trying to match-make her. Single life was fun. Besides, anyone who they would find wouldn't impress her mother. The man who won her mother's heart had to have a little magic up his sleeve.

"Oh, Susan, there's one for you." Her friend Elsie pointed to a handsome man who had walked in and was in line to order a drink.

"Oh, no, no, no, no. I'll find my own man, thank you very much."

"Oh come on, Susan. Go talk to him. What can it hurt?"

"My pride? You know I can't talk to men like that. I end up stumbling over my own tongue."

"True. I have heard how suave you can be when talking to the opposite sex." Her friend Cathy giggled. "Remember the last guy we pushed her on? What was it you said? I really like your crotch? When you meant to say you really liked his tie? I never laughed so hard."

"Yeah. Gave me the confidence boost I needed. Thanks." She raised her cup in a mock salute.

"Ladies, this has been fun, but I have to get home. My husband has been watching our children long enough." Elsie stood. "I'll see everyone tomorrow at work."

"We should be going too, Susan. I've got some work to do before we go in tomorrow."

Susan was happy to get out of there. She headed out to Cathy's car. Susan could walk home. Her apartment wasn't that far but the bitter cold had her catching a ride with her friend instead of walking.

119

"I'll drop you off in front of your apartment then go find a parking place and come up. Okay?" asked Cathy.

"Sure. It's still early. See you in a few." She dashed to the building and up the stairs. The warmth of her apartment was her only thought. She opened the door to her place and sighed as the heat blanketed around her. It was one of the best things about apartment living. It didn't take much to heat the place.

Something flickered out of the corner of her eye. "Oh, no."

There, floating in the face of her large wall mirror was a bunch of words written in flame. "How the heck am I supposed to get rid of that?"

She ran to her linen closet and grabbed a cloth. Once she was back at the mirror, she found she had grabbed a hand towel. "Oh yeah, that's going cover a lot."

Racing back to her closet she threw the offending towel back in and grabbed a sheet. It didn't matter what the sheet was as long as it covered the mirror. Just as she adjusted the sheet to make sure it covered the whole thing, her girlfriend knocked on the door then opened it.

"Found a spot right up front this time." She plopped onto the couch. Looking at the mirror, her brow furrowed. "You in mourning?"

"What?" Susan refused to look at the mirror. Maybe that wasn't what her friend was staring at.

"The covering over the mirror? That can mean a death in the family. Nice pattern too. Didn't know you were into Scooby Doo that much."

"No." She didn't pay attention to what she grabbed. Now she wished she did. "Just, um, it's dirty and I didn't want anyone to see it until I get it clean."

One corner started to slip off. Susan ran to the mirror to make sure it stayed put. "It will be fine once I clean it."

"Where's the glass cleaner?"

"Why?" Susan pulled on the other corner, which was trying to come loose as well.

Because if it bothers you that much then clean it now."

"No. I'm fine. I'll get to it later." She adjusted the cloth once more before joining her friend on the couch. She pasted a fake smile on her face. "Would you like something to drink?"

"It's okay. I really should be going now." Cathy stood and headed to the door. She pointed to the mirror. "Let me know when it's safe to come back in."

Susan knew she had freaked out her friend again, but she'd rather have them think she was a little *out there* than to try to explain she had magical powers. She walked her friend to the door. "I'll see you tomorrow then."

She sighed as she locked the door. Why did her friends put up with her? She grabbed all her glamour magazines and spread them out in front of her on the floor. Tomorrow she'll hear the jokes about her obsessing about the dirtiness of the mirror.

If only she could tell them her deep dark secret. Maybe they'd leave her alone if they knew.

She pulled the cotton sheet off the mirror. It held her attention as words written in flames filled it once again.

Student assignment due next class: Animation—you are to animate any object. One limitation—can't have been alive before. No old pets or relatives.

"What? I have to animate something for Saturday night's class? Are they crazy? I haven't mastered the other lessons they've made me do."

"What do you expect, my dear." The picture of her mother sitting on the coffee table came alive. She had a simple living room, a couch, and a love seat, a coffee-table, which was nothing more than a trunk she used for storage, but it was nice and flat on top and she loved the shine of the wood. The large mirror was on one wall and a thirty-two inch plasma television on the other. In fact, the picture of her mom was the only picture she kept out of her family and she had kept it because of her mother's insistence.

"Mom, why must you invade my privacy like this." She used her foot and shoved all the magazines under the couch. It took a couple of swipes. It surprised her when her mom didn't comment. "You need to use a front door like other parents."

"Umph." She stepped out of the small frame and adjusted her skirt before she sat on the couch. "You worry too much. No one will ever know of our little talent unless you tell them. I know better and have been at this a lot longer than you."

"Still, I am living in their world. We need to follow their rules." She went into her small kitchen and pulled out two cups. One was a typical teacup. The other had the distinct look of a real lemon. It was one of her goof-ups in class but she loved the lemony flavor and as long as the cup remained, she would use it. She came out with tray filled with cups, tea and coffee bags, and a pot. "Coffee or tea?"

"Tea, of course." Her mother took a cup and a tea bag. "I see you are still using your little badge of honor."

"I like my cup." Susan poured water into her lemon cup before doing the same for her mother. "Oh damn, I forgot the sugars and the cream."

"Don't worry sweetheart, I only need honey." She pulled a small bottle out of her purse. "Would you like to use some?"

"Sure." After taking a sip, she sighed. "I do miss having you around, Mom."

"You could come home anytime." Her mother stirred her tea three times before tapping the spoon against the cup. "I don't really understand why you want to live amongst these humans anyway."

"Mom, I've explained it over and over. I like it here. Now let's talk about my newest assignment." She gestured toward the mirror with the glowing words still floating there. "What exactly do they mean?"

"Use your imagination, darling." Her mother took a sip of her tea. "Is there something you wish to create? I mean you can use anything, a teapot, a chair, a baby doll. The only limit you have with this is you."

"Anything?"

"Of course." Her mother smiled. "You are my daughter so I expect it to be one of your best. Make me and your father proud."

"Yes, Mom." She took a sip of her tea. She pointed to the glowing words on her mirror. "How long will those stay there?"

"Until you tell them to go away. How did you get rid of them before?"

"This is the first time my assignment wasn't given in class. I had to throw a sheet over them to keep the words hidden."

"That explains the lovely Scooby-Do pattern on your floor."

Susan stood up and approached the mirror. She looked like she had flames dancing in her auburn hair. Her green eyes were a lot like her mothers but that was where the resemblance ended. Her mother had an olive complexion where Susan was fair. She focused on the words. "Go away?"

"You must be more forceful than that dear." Her mother gestured with her cup. "The command must be strong enough to break the magic that created the image."

She nodded. Facing the mirror once again, she squared her shoulders and said, "Go away."

The image faded from sight. The fact it worked put a smile on her face. Her magic wasn't the strongest of the family. That honor went to her sister, her precious, perfect sister. "Mom, I'm going to do my best, but I'm very new at this."

"I know you came into your powers very late but you're a Dent after all." Her mom took another sip of her tea.

That was a stigma to her. First, she had not developed powers when her siblings did, then when she did her powers wasn't up to the caliber the rest of the family had. It was hard being a late bloomer.

"Do you have any ideas?"

"For my assignment? Not really. Haven't had time to think about it." She sat back on the couch.

"Perhaps I could help you come up with something?"

Her mother would come up with some elaborate plan that she could never complete. Better to stop her mother before she got her claws into it. "I should do it myself. It's the only way I'm going to learn."

"You're right of course, but I thought I could help you come up with your project. Your sister and I had so much fun brainstorming on her projects." She sighed at the memory. "I do miss her."

"I know, mom. I do too." Susan patted her mom's hand.

"Even though you get compared to her all the time?"

"I know she was the perfect daughter." Susan smiled. "Never argued with you or dad, always had the highest grades, graduated best in her class but she was my best friend growing up. She protected me from those who wanted to make fun of me because of my lack of power."

"You know your uncle Vernon came to his powers late."

"Yes. I know, mom. He turned out to be the most powerful wizard of all. Ran the ruling council. I have heard the story many times. And as much as I'd love to live up to everyone's expectations I'm not banking all my hopes on it."

"I could always call your sister and have her come back to help you."

"Now you're just being mean. I can do this."

"You never know what you can accomplish when you put your heart in it." Her mom stood up. "But since you do have some homework to do I'll leave you to it."

"Love you, Mom." She gave her mom a kiss and watched as she stepped back into the picture. "If you need me, all you have to do is call me."

"Yes, ma'am." Once she was sure her mother wasn't in the picture anymore she pulled all the magazines back out and spread them around. She had started looking at the magazine to see the latest styles but now she stared without really focusing.

She thought her biggest concern was her friends making a fuss over her lack of a boyfriend. It didn't hold a candle to what she had to do now. How was she going to come up with something to animate that wouldn't be too lame. The family heritage made it worse. She couldn't disappoint the family.

The glossy images of beautiful women staring up at her from ads made her mind start to whirl. What about animating a picture? Her mom stepped out the frame, why couldn't she take a picture like the ones in front of her?

She smiled. That was what she would do. Now she had to figure out what she wanted to animate. "Hey, that would be cute." One of the ads had a fish bowl on it.

"Hmm." Maybe not, she wasn't sure if she could just make part of the picture move. There was a lot of things going on in the picture and if she made a mistake she could activate the wrong thing. She flipped the page. "Wow."

Crystal blue eyes stared at her. She didn't care for his hair but he had the prettiest eyes. As she flipped through the magazine she found herself looking at all the male models, but none of them were what she was looking for.

"The perfect man doesn't exist anyway." She closed her magazine and leaned back against the couch. A smile spread across her face. "But I could create him."

She scooped up her magazines and darted into her bedroom where her desktop was. It only took a few seconds to get her scanner warmed up. Picture after picture she scanned into her computer. Once she felt she had all the images she needed she started to piece parts of the pictures together.

The crystal blue eyes were the first thing she picked. They were her favorite. Then she found a nice full mouth she liked, a strong jaw line, eyebrows. Slowly she built her perfect man. She sat back and grinned at the hodgepodge image. "Not the prettiest thing I've seen.

"But something I can fix after I freshen up my tea." She went into the kitchen and added more hot water then her used tea bag. She stood there waiting for the tea to seep as she thought about what she was going to do next. Her computer held several programs that allowed her to alter pictures. One of them had to work. "But is all I want is a talking head? I am my mother's daughter."

She took a sip of her tea and thought. Then she snapped her fingers. "I need a manikin."

She leaned against the counter and thought for a moment as she took a sip of tea. After setting her coffee down, she opened her junk drawer and pulled out her wand. It didn't look like much, but she knew it helped focus her power. Before, when she tried spells, the power went everywhere. One time she tried to put rabbit ears on a bust of her father and she ended up putting real rabbit ears on every relative who happened to be in the room. It took hours for her to reverse the magic.

That was when her mom decided she needed a wand. Most of her friends who had seen it thought she had a strange stirring stick. It was fine with her as long as they didn't try to use it. The magic in it had a way of getting into the liquid stirred. One time she wasn't fast enough and she had friends with donkey ears and lion tails. It wasn't easy to explain and she didn't want to go through it again.

Susan tapped the wand against her hand. Little sparks of magic rained down on her floor. Small flowers bloomed for a few seconds before disappearing. "Let's see. I need to be creative, I need to be smart, I need to make a body to complete my art. Make him strong, make him tall. Don't worry about the face that's my job. If I do a good job I'll call him Bob." She twirled the wand and pointed it at her couch. "Hey I rhymed. Last time I did that, things didn't go so well. Sure hope this works."

A spark came out of the wand, centered over the couch and shimmered as it created something. It fluctuated and grew. Slowly it came together into two arms, two legs a torso, a head, a neck. Only one area remained smooth. "He looks like a Barbie Doll. Gotta fix that."

She sort of giggled as she looked at the manikin she made. "He needs a little something, something." This is a colloquial thing—I'd like to leave it in.

She tapped her wand against her palm. Little sparks came out of the tip each time. "Okay. So how do I word this? What rhymes with anatomically correct?"

"Here goes." She held out her wand and closed her eyes. "Spirits near and spirits far come answer my calling. I need your love and strength to create. You have been there for my ancestors. Be here for me."

She could feel the power build inside her. They were there to help her with the spell. Now she had to weave the spell itself. "Tonight I ask for your favor so I may bring life to this creation of mine. I need a real man. One who will bring this body to life. I wish for him to have a bright smile and a quick wit. To be handsome and smart. I also wish him to be built like a man one hundred percent.

She thought about going into details but then thought better of it. She'd be happy if he actually came alive. Even if it was for just a few minutes. "Thank you for your love and your strength. Thank you with your gift of magic. Thank you for your faith."

She bowed her head as the energy that had been building in her grew. Once she couldn't handle it anymore she opened her eyes and focused on her creation. Her wand dipped down and pointed at it. A shot of magic energy shot out and surrounded her new man.

Susan held her breath as the magic worked its way into her project. It had to work. It just had to.

~ * ~

Warren stood in front of the board of directors with a smile on his face. He hated this part of being the head of the council but he had a job to do. "Gentlemen and ladies, it is good to see you again."

"You can keep the pleasantries," answered one. "You have news?"

"Yes. Susan Dent has come into her magic." He knew they wouldn't be happy with his news.

"What are we going to do? Her family is too strong for us to control. Look at how much power and wealth we've been able to acquire since her grandfather passed. I thought we bound her abilities when she was an infant."

He had thought the same thing. "It doesn't matter. She has been taking magic classes and so far has not been a strong student."

"Her strength isn't important. It takes three children from magical parents who have their magic to challenge the board. There haven't been three children to have magic in years. The Dents are the first. Level of power doesn't matter when she has a sister and a brother who are both powerful."

"We must be sure—" He felt a weird sensation wash over him before his body felt like it was being pulled in a million different directions. A loud popping sound went off in his ears and his world went black.

~ * ~

Susan watched the spell settled on her man. His crystal blue eyes looked even better in person. His fill lips had a nice rose tinge to them.

"Oh, my. It worked?" She couldn't believe it. Her man blinked.

"It worked." A big grin broke across her face as she did a little jig. "Now what am I going to call you? Bob wouldn't work. You're not battery operated."

She snapped her fingers. "I know I'll call you Mac. My animated creation. That is a great title for my project."

"Something isn't quite right." Susan bit her lip as he sat there and stared at her. He showed no movement other than blinking. "I know. He's not talking."

~ * ~

Warren stared at the young woman who had been the center of his previous conversation before he lost consciousness. Where was he anyway? He couldn't move. No matter how hard he tried, he found his body planted on the couch and he couldn't lift a finger. She held her wand in her hand, tapping it against one palm. Didn't she know how dangerous that was? It was one of his first lessons and a hard one at that. The family cat didn't like being the victim of stray magic either and turning it into half a frog just pissed it off. It took the cat months to forgive him.

He felt the energy of the spell seep into him. Then he found he could speak, but she must have put limitations on the spell because he found he could only respond to her questions.

Susan sat opposite of him, on her coffee table, grinning like a Cheshire cat. She was proud of herself. She sat her wand down, jumped up and clapped her hands together. "This is too cool!"

How did she trap him like this anyway? He felt a slight breeze from the heater kicking on and shifted his gaze down. The only thing he found he could move was his eyes. Good Lord, he was naked. What the hell was going on?

Susan walked out of the room and came back with a bundle of cloth. "I don't have any men's clothing but we can fix that tomorrow. All I have for you right now is a sweat suit. Hope you don't mind."

He heard himself say. "I don't mind." But he did mind. If he could move his arms, he'd strangle her.

She dropped the clothes next to him. "You can dress yourself, right?"

He wanted to say only if she wished him to, but it didn't fall into the parameters of her spell. New wizards didn't understand the restrictions of spells and often let out the small nuances that allowed the spells to work without having to be corrected.

When he didn't move she seemed to understand. She picked up her wand from the coffee table. "Now let's see. You need to be able to interact with other people and take care of your own basic functions so I need to be sure you have some independence, but I can't let you run wild through the city so I have to do this right."

He had a few choice words but could only think them.

"Oh great ancestors one more time, please. Mac needs to be able to act like a real person. Be able to eat, drink, and dress himself. I need to be able to take him out into public until my project is due, but he will obey me in everyway." She pointed her wand at him and waited. "Thank you once again, oh, and I promise to do better with these spells as I get use to this."

Another stream of magic flowed into him. His fingers flexed as his body started to move.

"Well, go on. Get dressed." She smiled at him sweetly, like she had no clue what her magic was doing to him.

He grabbed the sweatshirt and hauled it over his head. The sleeves only covered three fourths of his arms. The pants weren't any better, but at least the rest of his body was covered.

Susan moved about the room effortlessly. Clueless to the pain she was inflicting. How dare she trap him like this and act so innocent? He forced his body to stand up and took a few steps toward her before his feet got hooked up in some throw rug on her floor and he went down like a statue. He couldn't even put his arms out to soften the fall. His body slammed into the floor with so much force he was surprised when he didn't crash through to the apartment below.

"Oh my!" Gentle warm hands touched his cumbersome trap, checking for injuries before helping him roll over. "You okay?"

He looked at the concern in her eyes. How did she make it seem so real? Once again, he found he had to answer to her will. He nodded and smiled back at her.

Her face softened as she helped him to his feet. "I guess I should have given you a little grace as well, but I'm afraid to ask my ancestors to help any more. I'll have to help you watch where you walk instead. Make sure that doesn't happen again."

Her comment didn't require a response so he found he couldn't talk. If he could, what would he be able to say anyway? He felt resigned to follow her desires until the spell ended. He was pretty sure she didn't set the spell so it would never end. Maybe if she said enough he'd know how and when the spell would fall apart and could prepare himself.

She continued what she was doing, digging in a closet and pulling out items that heaped at her feet. "I'm getting a little tired so we need to go to bed. Since you're my first animated creation I'm not sure where you should sleep. Your fall a few minutes ago makes me think the floor might be a better place for you."

A pillow and a blanket dropped to the floor at his feet. He sure hoped she'd say something about him picking it up or it would sit there all night.

Susan turned from him again. His imaginary jaw dropped as her shirt hit the floor. What was she doing? She continued to shed her clothes, allowing him a prime view of her luscious body.

He had been watching her for several months but never suspected what she hid under all the clothes she wore. She loved the layered look. It must have been a safety mechanism. She hid her figure from herself and everyone else. Now that he a powerful view he had to wonder why?

If only he could talk. It would be the first question out of his mouth. He was grateful he was trapped in this manikin body because her beauty was affecting him. Even though he didn't have his own body he felt his being stiffen with desire. She was so beautiful. She slipped on a long cotton gown. Blocking his view and frustrating him immensely. The gown did nothing for her.

"Well, goodnight then." She climbed into her bed and lay down. It didn't take too long before she realized he still stood where she left him. "What's the matter?"

"You must command me."

"Oh." She sat up and puzzled at his answer. "Oh! Mac, please make your bed and lay down so you can rest."

His body bent to gather the items she heaped at his feet. Once he had spread them on the floor, he laid down.

She released a sigh of relief before lying back down. Susan clapped her hands together and the light went off. "I love the clapper."

He had no idea what a clapper was but felt glad the room had darkened. Now he had to figure out how to get out of his predicament. He'd lost his sense of direction when she was naked, but couldn't let a beautiful body distract him. The cotton crinkled as she shifted in the bed. Every time she moved, he imagined the body he had admired. What was wrong with him?

He didn't need this complication. Her breathing fell into a deep and even cadence. She must be asleep. He was tired but wasn't sure if her spell would allow him to sleep. He emptied his mind and relaxed his spirit so he could try to rest. Her even breathing helped him to relax even more, to where he felt he was floating. Random thoughts filtered in and out but nothing stuck. He drifted as the night deepened. Soft sounds from the living room brought him back to a state of alertness.

"Susan."

She stirred, but didn't wake up. Instead, she murmured a little and shifted in the bed. He heard the sheets sliding against her limbs.

"Susan." The voice got closer and its tone a little sharper. He wished he could move. She was being robbed and would sleep right through it.

She finally sat up in her bed, rubbing sleep from her eyes. "Mom?"

"God, you sleep deep. Turn on the light."

"Um, how about I come out to my living room?" She swung her feet out and stood up. She didn't need her mom finding a man sleeping on her floor. Right now, the darkness kept him hidden. "What are you doing here so late anyway?"

"Something has happened." Her mother's shadow fell across him as she stood in the doorway.

"What was so dire that you couldn't wait until tomorrow?" Susan padded around him. Making sure her mother wasn't aware of the mannequin on her floor.

"Warren has disappeared."

"Warren? The guy who is the head of the council? I thought he was the most powerful wizard amongst us. Maybe he just had a hot date." She stepped into the hallway.

"They said he disappeared right in front of their eyes. Someone more powerful must have done it."

"Okay." She ran her fingers through her hair. "What does that have to do with me?" Their voices started to fade when Susan offered her mom some tea.

~ * ~

Susan didn't want her mom to know about her project yet. She wanted it to be a surprise since she'd botched so many before. "Let's go to the living room. Want some tea?"

"No dear. I wanted to make sure you had all your protections up. If they can take him no one is safe."

"Mom. I have no real power, why would they come after me?"

"Our family has always been the most powerful. We ruled the council up until your grandfather."

"I know the story, Mom. We haven't been able to challenge the council because there hasn't been enough siblings until now. But don't the three siblings have to have enough power to activate some sort of globe? You know my power is almost non-existent." She held up her hand when her mother went to protest. Susan headed back to her bedroom. If her mother wasn't going to leave she needed something to keep her warm.

"You want to think I have this great amount of untapped power, Mom, but I know better. Why would we want to challenge the council anyway. You said they were doing a good job." Susan talked loud so her mother could hear her.

"They are." Her mom's voice grew louder when she came back into the hallway. "And that isn't why I brought up the point our family has been most powerful. Just because you don't feel you have a lot of power won't stop someone from trying to kidnap you."

"Oh come on, Mom." She stepped into the darkened room and walked to her closet. "You are too paranoid."

"I am not. We all believed your grandfather was killed but could never prove it. What if someone was trying to control the council? You could be the perfect pawn."

"How?" She pulled her house robe from the hanger and wrapped it around her shoulders.

"They could offer you the chance to grow your power."

"You have been reading too many spy books. If there was such a spell I would think everyone would want to get their hands on it. The council is good, but I don't think they could keep something like that a secret." She closed the closet door and walked back into the hallway.

"Are you cold, dear?"

"It's three thirty in the morning, what do you think?" She stifled a yawn.

~ * ~

Warren listened to the two of them. When they were further away he had to strain to catch the words, but then they came back into the room he had no problem hearing them. He was amazed at how close her mother had guessed at the council's plan. But he was surprised at their reaction to his disappearance. He was sure they planned it. Could it have been an accident because of a novice?

He mentally shook his head. If they had done it on purpose then they would know he was listening. They were very good, but he wasn't going to fall for it. They wandered down the hall again making him strain once again to hear anything they said. From what he could hear was more of the same.

It didn't take long for Susan to come back to her bed. She sighed as she sat down. A few seconds later, she stood and crossed to the small window near her dresser. "I wish I wasn't part of this family. I like living with the humans. I was quite happy without any of the family power."

He found that an odd statement.

~ * ~

Susan bent down and dragged a small box out from under the desk. Pulling out the items she needed, she set up her alter and lit two candles. Susan sat in front of her altar, closed her eyes and emptied her mind. It was time to thank her ancestors properly.

"Dear ancestors. Thank you for blessing me and my family. I am humbled by your love and protection." She sat in silence for a few moments after that. Thankful her family had such wonderful people who had lived before her. Their pure souls had always been there for her. "I will always follow your guidance. Continue to lead me in the right direction."

She glanced back at Mac. "And thank you so much for allowing me to not botch my creation. It turned out so much better than I expected. I didn't think it would be as lifelike as it is."

Susan prayed to her relatives a little longer then finished communing with them. She blew out the candles, but let them sit so they could cool. Standing, she looked around her room. Her big bed awaited her and she should be happy to climb back into it since she didn't get a lot of sleep, but she found it hard to get back into it. Her mother's odd appearance in her apartment in the middle of the night made her worry.

Could someone have it out for the family?

She really didn't want to go back to sleep. Her mind was going a mile a minute and not relaxed enough to rest. There was only one thing that would relax her now. Her vibrating buddy, Bob. She reached for her nightstand drawer then realized she wasn't alone.

Susan looked at Mac. Could she actually do what she was contemplating? Can he perform anyway? She sighed. There was only one way to find out.

"Mac. I don't want you to sleep on the floor anymore. Please climb into my bed." She could feel her body shaking. Why was she so nervous? He was hers to command.

And she made sure he was anatomically correct.

A giggle escaped her as she slipped her gown off.

Why was she feeling nervous? He wasn't real. And who would know anyhow? She was acting silly.

Mac stood and climbed into the bed. He showed no emotion as he lay on the bed but what did she expect? Big smiles and open arms?

She got in beside him and pulled the covers up to her chin. This was something she had never done before so she was feeling nervous. Taking a deep breath, she spoke softly. "Mac, I want to have sex with you."

Boy, that didn't sound pretty and there was no way to flower it up.

"Of course."

His statement had her giggling again. "You need to take your clothes off."

As he stood and undressed, she wondered if he could get it up. Not something she had thought about when she created him. Well, now she'll have to see just how detailed she made that spell. "Climb into my bed."

The fact that he obeyed her every word did have the wheels in her head turning. This can really work in her favor. "Turn toward me."

He shifted in the bed so he faced her.

Susan hesitantly pressed her right hand to his chest. "I can't believe I'm doing this."

His skin felt warm to her touch and she felt his heart beat. It surprised her. She hadn't expected that. "I don't know what I expected."

She also wasn't sure why she spoke to him the way she did. He wouldn't answer her unless she asked a direct question. Right now she wasn't sure if she wanted him talking back to her. He could suddenly tune into her conscious and she wasn't sure she wanted that. At least not right now.

But it meant she had to do everything herself. Bob was one thing, but a manikin? She wasn't sure if she could do it but she sure was going to try. "Touch me."

"Yes." Mac placed a finger on her chin and then pulled it back.

That wasn't going to work. She had to think this through a little more. Mac would do what she wanted, but not the way she wanted unless she was explicit.

"I want you to touch me here." She placed her hand on her breast, cupping it the way she wanted him to cup her. "And keep it there."

He placed his hand on her breast the way she showed him. "Good. Now roll onto your back."

He followed her command, which gave her a chance to see if he could be aroused. Susan gripped the base of him with one hand, gently squeezing him with her fingers. A smile filled her lips when she felt him harden. It would work. She worked her hand up and down his shaft, stroking him to get him to harden. It felt like silk in her hands turning to steel very quickly.

Just what the doctor ordered. She climbed on top of him once he was hard. Thank goodness no one could see what she was doing. Her vibrator was one thing, yet this was like having sex with a blow-up doll and she never thought she'd go that route. And for some reason she started feeling embarrassed.

His length slid inside her, bringing another smile to her face. It felt good. Much better than bob. She pumped her body up and down his shaft. He was just the right size for her, not too big, not too small, not too thick, not too thin. How she got that right, she wasn't sure but she was grateful.

Her breath hitched as she picked up her tempo. As she moved up and down him faster, she felt the sensations intensify. It started slowly. A gentle flush to her skin, her heart picked up its beat a tempo. Then her muscles contracted and goosebumps rose on her arms. She knew she was getting close. Picking up the pace, she threw her head back as she tightened her muscles against him, squeezing him in a vice like grip. She felt every movement they made. Sensations of joy washed over her. "Almost."

The words floated in the air. She grabbed his hands and changed their position. "Pinch them just a little."

His fingers pinched her nipples. "Oh, man. That's it."

Her body spasmed, her muscles tightened and she soared.

~ * ~

The next morning she sat at her table drinking a hot cup of coffee. She loved the smell of it brewing in the morning. Mac was still in the bedroom. When she left, he still had his eyes closed. Probably something she said before she fell asleep. The sun peeked its way into her tiny apartment, bathing her in warm sunlight. Closing her eyes, she allowed the rays to bathe her. Man, she loved the feeling.

Now she had to figure out what to do with Mac. Last night she learned he could perform, but only what she asked of him. There had to be a better way to do this. She didn't want to do all the work all the time. Her phone rang, startling her out of her thoughts.

"Hello?"

"Susan. Good, you're home. I was afraid you'd already be on your way to work."

She looked at her clock. "I don't normally leave for about an hour and you know that Beth." Was she crazy? The hairs on the back of her neck stood up. Oh, no. They must be planning some sort of blind date. "What are you up to?

"Me and the girls were thinking about getting together for dinner. You up for it?" There was a slight hint of fear in her voice.

"I'd love to." She paused for a moment. A smile crept across her face. This was going to feel good. "But I have company in town so I'll have to turn you guys down. Sorry."

"Bring her along." Beth's voice cracked a little.

"It's a guy." She felt it hang between them, wondering what her friend was thinking.

"Bring him."

Bring him? Not the answer she expected. Can she take Mac into public? This would be a true test of her magic. "Let me talk to him and see what sort of plans he has made. I'll let you know later on today."

"Okay. Sure."

Susan hung up the phone with a big grin on her face. This might be the first time she had the last laugh and she was enjoying it. She poured herself another cup of coffee and headed to her bedroom. It only took a few minutes for her to get dressed.

Then she looked at Mac. He still lay on the bed where she left him. "So what shall I do with you while I'm at work? Can't have you underfoot, but I'm worried my mom will try to come back and spy on my protection spells while I'm not home."

Her eyes lit up when she came up with the perfect idea.

Once she was ready to head to work, she brought Mac out of her bedroom. "You should be safe enough without me. I don't want you to move. If you need to get something to eat or need to use the bathroom that's fine. You can even turn on the television if you get bored, but do not leave this apartment. Don't answer the phone unless you hear my voice on the answering machine, and please hide if my mother figures out a way to get into my apartment. She can't know you exist." With that, she grabbed her mother's picture, her bag and headed out the door.

~ * ~

Mac stared at the door for a few moments before he realized she had really left him alone. Now he had time to figure out how to get out of here without Susan watching over him all the time. He knew her commandments would keep him trapped in the small room he sat in until he could break the spell but he planned on breaking the spell before she got back.

He tried to focus on the task at hand, but his mind kept wandering back to what transpired between them last night. No one had ever taken advantage of him before and this woman knew no bounds. She trapped him in this body then forced him to have sex with her. Although he had to admit, he had enjoyed her little show. The fact he had wanted to participate a little more than she had allowed surprised him.

~ * ~

Susan was focused on the project she had been assigned.

"Susan, um, your purse is, um, jumping," commented one of her coworkers.

"What?" It took a few seconds before the words truly penetrated her brain.

She grabbed her purse and headed to the bathroom. Her purse was jerking violently in her hands by the time she had locked the main door and made it into the small stall in the bathroom. The purse banged against the wall of the stall several times before she finally gained enough control to open it. She pulled the picture of her mother out of her purse.

"I wondered why you had been so adamant about where I put this picture." She placed the picture on the counter.

Her mother stepped out of the frame and started pacing in the small room. "I can't believe you took my picture to work with you."

"I can't believe you were going to go into my apartment while I was at work. You have no respect for me?" Susan jammed her hands on her hips. "I took the picture because I knew you didn't trust my ability to protect my apartment."

Her mom stopped pacing. "That isn't true."

"Then why are you here now?"

"Because I was worried." She placed her hands on her daughter's arms. "I do have faith in you, but I also know what lengths they went to when your great grandfather was killed. I only meant to help. My thought was to protect you, not question your ability."

"Mom, how am I to learn if you don't let me do this myself?" Susan returned the gesture. "I know you care, but I have done my studies and I'd like to think I can handle something simple like a protection spell. You taught them to me when I was a child. I didn't have to have any magical powers to do the spell either."

"I'm sorry. I can't help it. You're my baby."

"I'm full grown."

A loud banging vibrated in the little room.

Susan looked at the door. "Mom, you have to go."

"Tap on the screen and I'll pop by later."

She gave her mom a kiss and just about pushed her into the picture. Before her mother's image settled on the photo she shoved it into her oversized purse and opened the door. "Sorry."

The woman gave Susan an odd look as she slipped past her, giving her an arched brow as Susan clutched her purse closer to her chest. The woman probably thought she was afraid she'd steal the purse but she had her reasons. She didn't know what would happen if her mom's picture fell out and crashed to the carpet. How would she explain her mother suddenly popping into existence? She didn't want to take the chance.

~ * ~

She walked into her apartment and found Mac right where she left him. He was better than a pet. Now she had to decide if she wanted to take Mac out into public. It would be a test of her magic. And it could get her friends off her back for a while.

"Mac, we're going out with my friends." She sat in a chair opposite from where he sat on the couch. "We need to get you some clothes first. So do we do this the human way or the magic way?"

He just looked at her.

"Magic it is." She picked up several of her magazines to see what the male models wore in the advertisements. There had to something she could create for him. The only spell she knew was the 'silk out of a sow's ear' which meant she had to find some old clothes to convert to his new ones. "Mac. I need you to take off your clothes."

He stood and peeled off the sweatshirt and pants she had given him.

"Thanks." She laid them on the floor next to the picture she had chosen. A pair of jeans with a button-down white blouse and a tweed jacket. A quick dash into her kitchen and her wand was in hand and ready to caste the spell.

"Now. How did this go?" She tapped the wand on her teeth. "Oh, right. Keep it simple and true. "Great spirits I need your help. I need to change these simple threads to the cloths on this page."

That was simple enough. A smile spread across her mouth when the jersey material started to shimmer and shift. It only took seconds for the clothing to change. She picked up the clothing and handed it to Mac. "Here you go."

Mac took the clothing from her.

"Get dressed." She had to do something about him doing exactly what she told him and no more. That won't work with her friends. In two seconds they'd catch on there was something wrong and throw him to the wolves.

"Mac." He had just buttoned the cuffs to the shirt she had recreated for him. "You will be meeting friends of mine who will not be very nice to you if you behave the way you have been. I need you to think for yourself, react to what people say and do around you. You need to act like every other male out there. Not nearly as obnoxious though. You need to show class, be sweet. Be yourself."

~ * ~

She said the magic words. Now he could actually talk to her, ask her questions. Figure out how to break the spell. He gloated for the few moments when she went into her bedroom to change her clothes but the moment she stepped back into the room he forgot all about his thoughts of freedom.

The short hot pink dress she had donned made his heart stop for a minute. Why did she hide those gorgeous legs? He followed her out the door of her apartment, down the stairs and out into the bitter cold. There were a few perks to being trapped in a manikin. He couldn't feel the cold like she could.

She started walking down the street. It took him a few steps to catch up. "We're walking?"

"Yes. It's only a few buildings down. One of the reasons I moved to this part of the city. I don't have to own a car." She pulled her coat tighter around her. "By the way, please don't do anything to make me look like a fool. My friends can be a little vicious from time to time."

"They don't know about your powers?" She bound him from using her friends against her. Damn. It was a way to get her to release him from the spell.

"Good gravy, no. Are you kidding? There's no way to know how someone would react if they knew about them and I sure don't want to end up stuck in my family's world. I like it here." She stopped in front of a door. "Here we are. Now, you're a friend of the family. My mom set us up on a date."

They entered the establishment and were inundated by noise. The sound assaulted his ears. *How did she put up with this?*

140

"Over there." Susan pointed to the three women waving at them. "Put on your game face. It could get bumpy."

He found her comment strange. If these women were so bad, why did she hang out with them?

The three women waiting for them stood when they came up to the table and gave Susan a hug. They did it as a group, not caring what anyone thought. It sure looked a little strange to him.

"Susan, you must introduce your friend."

"This is Mac. A friend of the family. Um, he's in town visiting and my mother thought it would be a good idea to show him around." Susan gestured to the chair next to the one she took. He took the chair and sat down.

"Does he talk?"

Susan swallowed. "Of course. Mac, don't be afraid to talk to them. They don't bite. Much."

"Good evening, Ladies." He gave them his best smile, not knowing how well it translated through the manikin. "It's a pleasure to meet all of you."

"Oh, the pleasure is ours." The one who spoke had short spiky brown hair, definitely into designer clothes and a calculating look in her eyes. *What was she thinking about?*

"So, you're friends with our Susan?" asked another.

"Sorry. Where are my manners? This is Elsie, and that is Cathy. And the one who keeps staring at you is Beth." She pointed to the women who sat to her left, then the one across from them then to the one who had spoken first.

So Beth was the calculator in designer clothes. Cathy, sweet, young, and with long blonde hair she had in a flip, looked like a woman who wanted to be Suzy Homemaker. She wore a cute little flower dress that looked like she stepped out of a 1950's magazine. Elsie was had jet black hair with several strands of fuchsia. Her wild outfit made him wonder. Bold colors, ripped tights and high top sneakers. It didn't seem to fit the calm woman who sat there.

He nodded. "Yes, I am friends with your Susan." He said to Cathy. "How long have you known her?"

"Oh, about two years. The four of us met at the office when we first started. We were all newbies and gravitated together. Been friends ever since." Cathy grabbed Susan's hand and gave it a squeeze.

At least this one had real affection for Susan.

"Susan has been there for all of us," said Beth. "She is a wonderful person and we only want what's best for her."

"So I'm under the magnifying glass until I gain your approval?"

"Yes," all four said it in unison.

"Guys." Susan turned a deep shade of red. "You don't have to be so honest. You could get me into trouble."

Why?" asked Beth. "I think your mom would appreciate that we're trying to protect you."

"Believe me she would, but I'd appreciate it if you wouldn't protect me with such zest. It's a little embarrassing to have three women drilling the first man I've ever brought around them. He might find it a little bit disconcerting."

"Sorry. We only have your best interests at heart." Beth gave her a sympathetic smile. "Mac, forgive us."

He nodded.

"So how do you know Susan?" asked Elsie.

He had to smile. If nothing, they were persistent. "Her family and mine have known each other for several generations." It was the truth, just not one she knew. "I came into town to visit and her mom didn't want me to get bored, so asked Susan to show me around. How's that?"

He got a genuine smile in return. "So you've known Susan all your life?"

"Yes." It wasn't a lie, considering she had just created him. It should keep her happy and that was one of the things she had asked him to do.

"Isn't she the sweetest person?" Elsie gushed.

He nodded. Warren wanted to say how he really felt. That he suspected she was plotting to bring her family to power and really didn't care who she hurt, but he had to follow her perimeters.

"Elsie, please."

"Oh, come on. He deserves to know how wonderful you are. You were there for me when my grandfather died. You didn't even know him and helped me with the funeral arrangements. I couldn't have done it without you."

"I didn't do anything out of the ordinary. This was the man who raised you when your parents died. You had no other family when he passed and you were too upset over his death to be able to get the job done." The heat of another blush filled her cheeks. Susan wondered how bad it showed.

"Then there was the time I needed money to visit my Nana when she fell and broke her hip. You lent me the money even though you couldn't really afford it." Beth put her hand on top of Susan's. "When I found out you couldn't pay your rent for the month I wanted to kick myself. I should have known you didn't really have it."

"I knew you were good for it, and my landlord understood." She kept her gaze down. He could hear the embarrassment in her voice. "Let's change the subject before you nominate me for sainthood."

"Sure."

Silence fell around the little table for a few minutes.

"You know he reminds me of someone." Beth sat back in her seat and studied Mac.

"Really?" Susan looked over at Mac. Who could he possibly look like? She didn't try to model him after anyone.

Beth snapped her fingers. "I know. He looks like the guy standing next to your mom in the picture she had hanging over the fireplace at your house."

Susan frowned. Her friends had only been to her mom's house one time. How the heck did Beth remember that picture? Of course she had spent the entire time they were there making sure no magic was used around them. It had kept her kind of busy. She thought about the picture.

The man in picture came into view in her mind. The moment it did, she saw the resemblance. Great googly moogly. He did. What was the man's name? As much as she racked her brain, she couldn't remember. Then another thought entered her mind. Would modeling him after someone from the magical realm affect her grade? The moment her thoughts wavered so did her spell on his clothes. She placed a hand on his arm and felt jersey. Her head whipped around fast enough to give her whiplash to see his sleeve. She saw the bottom of the sleeve had converted back to the sweatshirt but the top was still the jacket.

Susan squeezed her eyes closed and repeated the spell again. She never forgot her spells. Most wrote their spells down and kept them in a book and she knew one day she would probably have to start doing that. She hadn't created that many and they hadn't all been that successful. The sleeve converted to jacket material and she breathed a sigh of relief.

"You okay, Susan?"

"What?" She jerked her head toward the voice and felt something cold and wet splash against her neck before she felt it slide down her collarbone and down into her dress.

"Moved a little too much, huh?" she asked as she fished an ice cube out of her ear.

"I am so sorry, Ma'am." The young woman delivering their drinks blabbered. She sat the now empty tray on the floor and proceeded to try to wipe Susan down.

"Don't." She reached out and grabbed the woman's hand. "It's not your fault. Please just tell me there wasn't any red wine in the mix."

"I'm sorry."

"It's okay." Her outfit was ruined and it was one of her favorites. "I hate to do this but I can't eat all sticky like this. Can you cancel my meal and my friend's here?"

"Oh, no."

"Please don't blame yourself. This is still my favorite restaurant. But I have things sticking in places that make me uncomfortable. I need to change." She stood up. "Where's that tray?"

The waitress had it in her hand.

"Thanks."

"Susan, you coming back?" Beth asked as she stood.

"I don't think so. By the time I get to my apartment, shower, and change you'll be done. Let's try this again some other time." She looked around to see if anyone overheard her. "And I'll make sure I bring my raincoat."

She headed out the door once she was sure Mac followed her and headed back to her apartment. Thank goodness she didn't live far. Her shoes squished as she walked.

~ * ~

Susan stood under the spray of the hot shower, enjoying the water as it cascaded down her body. She had thought to bring Mac into the shower with her, have one night of fun before she confronted the fact that she recreated someone from the magical realm and it could cause problems. She was too afraid he'd melt to a gelatinous blob pooled at her feet.

It was time to get out so she turned the knobs to the off position and stepped out to the steamy room. Her hand grabbed the fluffy towel she had set aside to dry herself off with. Once done she set it aside and donned her bathrobe. Taking her brush, she ran it through her hair until all the knots were out. Hair covered her. "I shed like a sheepdog."

She opened door to the hallway, bracing herself for the coolness of the apartment. The bathroom was so nice and toasty she could stay there for hours but she had company and she had plans for that company.

Mac sat on the couch where she left him. "Feel better?"

"Much. I feel all squeaky clean." She wasn't quite sure how to let him know what was on her mind. He seemed so real since she gave him permission to talk freely.

"Good." He stood up and took her hands in his. "Ready for bed?"

That wasn't what she expected. "Um, yes as a matter of fact I am."

"Good." He released one hand and headed back to her bedroom. "Can I ask one thing, this time?"

"Sure."

"Can I be in control?"

"Um." Susan didn't know what to say. "Sure."

He tightened his grip on her hand for a moment. Mac stopped in front of the bed then turned to face her.

She stood there hesitantly. Not real sure what she should do. He smiled at her as he took her into his arms. Her heart fluttered in her chest. His lips pressed against hers, chaste, sweet.

Susan couldn't help but smile. Her manikin probably didn't really know what to do. He surprised her when his mouth slanted against hers and his tongue brushed against the seam of her lips, asking for entrance. She gave it easily. The sensation of his tongue dancing with hers sent heated excitement through her. Cool air brushed against her skin as he eased the robe off her shoulders. It pooled on the floor at her feet.

He broke the kiss and gave her a smile. Mac maneuvered her to the edge of the bed and eased her down. The soft comforter embraced her as she sank into it. She felt his weight press into her when he lay on top of her. Heat from his body enveloped hers. It felt so good. Her hands slid up his stomach. She made good magic.

Of course so did he. His hands had been busy, skimming across her body. She felt the warmth of his fingers brush against the underside of her breast before they cupped her. She moaned when he pinched her tips ever so gently. She wrapped her legs around him. Waiting anymore wasn't an option. She wanted him inside her and now.

He entered her quickly at her urging, causing her to sigh in satisfaction. He felt so good inside her. Mac started to move inside her, slow at first then faster as she met him thrust for thrust.

Her muscles tightened against him, taking him in a vice like grip and making his body shake. He was feeling it too. Something she didn't expect. Her body clinched as the sensations got stronger. She didn't know how much longer she could hold on. One stroke was all it took. She soared through the heavens as her orgasm hit. It was strong and all encompassing. "I'm sure going to miss this."

"Why?"

"Because once I show you to my teacher and get my grade I'm assuming the magic that created you will fall apart and you will cease to exist."

~ * ~

Susan slipped into a jogging suit before she readied herself to contact her mom. She picked up her mother's picture and tapped on the glass. It didn't take but a minute before her mother's image came to life.

"Darling, this isn't a good time." She stepped through the picture and brushed her hair from her face.

"What's wrong, Mom. It isn't my brother or sister is it?"

"Oh, no. Your sister and brother are fine. It's the disappearance of the councilman I told you about earlier, but it's nothing for you to be concerned about."

"Then do you have a few moments? I have a question and you're the only one I can ask."

"I guess." She stepped through the frame and sat on the couch.

"What's the problem?"

"I've created my project but I'm not sure it's politically correct. Will you look at it?"

"Of course."

"Thanks. I'll be right back." She stepped back to her room, took Mac's hand, and led him into the living room. Susan didn't say anything, she just stepped aside and watched her mother's reaction as she focused on Mac.

"What have you done?" Her mother stood slowly, like she was seeing someone coming back from the dead. "No wonder they think you did it."

"Did what? What are you talking about Mom?"

"Warren." Her mother turned to look at her. "That is Warren."

"No, no. I just created something that looks like him." Susan stood in front of Mac, protecting him from her mother's scrutiny. "I didn't have anyone in mind when I created Mac. There's no way my power was strong enough to do what you're saying. We both know that."

"Honey. You have to release him." Her mother gave her a sympathetic look. "I'm sorry, but you have to."

"But I haven't trapped anyone. Have I?" She turned to face Mac who nodded. "Oh, no. I didn't mean to."

"Go get your wand, dear," said her mother. "You must make this right."

Susan nodded and dashed into her kitchen. She came back with her wand. "Please know I'm sorry. I didn't know my magic had gone so wonky."

She closed her eyes for a moment before pointing her wand at him. "Magic is new to me and sometimes I don't know my own strength. I free you from this prison I didn't know I had created."

Magic shot out of the wand and circled Mac's body. Light blossomed around him, pulsing and shifting as her spell fell apart. Susan took several steps back to watch. The manikin body shrunk for a moment before exploding off him. The real man stood in his place. Naked.

"Um, you might want to put something on." Susan was now shielding her mother from him. But her mother didn't want to be shielded. "Mother, really!"

Warren looked down. "Oh, sorry." With a wave of his wrist he covered himself. A smile covered his lips as the magic settled into clothing.

She guessed he liked that a lot better than the sweat suit she had him all the time. Susan felt a weird sensation wrap around her before the apartment blurred and she found herself standing in a large chamber with big dark desks and a bunch of books.

"Warren, you're all right." The new voice to her right spoke. When she looked, she found herself in the council chambers.

"Of course." He straightened his clothes. "Why wouldn't I be?"

"We're sorry we didn't find you earlier but it took a while to follow the magic. It isn't easy in the mortal realm." One of the council members signaled to one of their guards. "But we can take it from here."

The guard took a hold of Susan's arm.

"Hey!" She tried to free herself but only made matters worse. She ended up in a strong body hold. One she couldn't get out of if she tried.

"Let her go." Warren stepped up to the guard and pulled her free.

"I don't understand." Susan said it, but so did several of the councilors and her mother. And they all said it at the same time.

"No one has asked me what happened. You're just assuming the worst." He kept a protective hand on her. "I know we were worried about the fact that this family could now challenge the council but that was before I got a chance to spend some quality time with Susan."

"But you disappeared in mid-sentence. Are you saying you weren't kidnapped?"

"Not on purpose," Susan blurted. She then slapped her hand over her mouth when Warren gave her a cross look.

"I had an opportunity to spend time with Susan and I took it." He stared at the council members. "You really think her magic was powerful enough to capture me?"

Susan turned to look at him. He squeezed her arm slightly. She hoped he would explain everything to her because she was pretty sure she had captured him and his words were confusing her.

"I wish to speak to Susan and her mother privately for a few moments. Then I will give you a full report."

"Of course." They filed out of the room.

"Mac?"

"The name is Warren."

She felt the heat of a blush fill her cheeks. "Sorry. Why did you tell them you weren't kidnapped? I mean I didn't do it on purpose, but I did do it."

"How do you think it would look for me to say a novice could overpower my magic? We're both safer if they believe I 'let' you capture me. It's one of the reasons I wanted to speak to you both alone. I can't have you contradicting me while I speak to these people."

"I don't understand." Susan's mom spoke up. "Why are you protecting my daughter?"

"Because I've gotten to know her." He took Susan's hand. "And I like what I've gotten to know."

He walked toward where the other council members waited for him with Susan in tow. Her mother not too far behind. "Gentlemen."

"You said you went to her?"

"Of course. She was assigned the animation assignment at her last class. One I set up. I stepped in when she tried to create her assignment."

They all nodded. No one would question him.

"Why did you decide to animate a manikin?"

"My mother." She looked at her mom then Warren before she looked at the man who asked her the question. "She kept throwing the family heritage in my face and I thought the life size animated man would please her and my teachers."

"Susan, you didn't need to prove yourself."

"Yes I did, Mom. Even though you never said it, you wanted me to be as good or better than my siblings. How many times have you reminded me about Uncle Vernon, the last bloomer?"

"I never meant to make you feel inadequate. I love you too much. It doesn't matter if you have any power at all, you're still my baby."

"Ladies, you can reconcile later." Warren interrupted them. "I just want my fellow council members to know that your family is no threat to them. You have no designs on trying to take over the council."

"What? No! I didn't want to have this power at all. Being human made me quite happy."

"And how do you feel about having a magical man in your life?"

"My whole family is magical." What an odd question.

He arched one brow at her. "I'm not talking about your family I'm talking about me."

"You? Oh." Wait he wanted to be with her, even after what she did to him? "Oh! You mean you want to be with me?"

"Yes. If you'll have me."

"But I don't have any power. You could have any woman you wanted, why me?" She felt her heart beat a little faster.

"Because you're different than anyone I've ever met." He kissed one eyelid. "Most women try to prove they're just as powerful as I am." He kissed another. "I've seen you for you." He kissed one cheek. "I have seen how big your heart is." Then another. "How much you care about those close to you." He kissed her gently on the lips. "You cared about me, even though you had no clue who I was." And a second time. "And I learned to care for you."

"Me?" She couldn't believe her voice squeaked.

"Yes. You." He placed his hands on either side of her face. "Now I feel this place is a little too crowded for us to continue this conversation."

Susan felt the world melt away from them. She found solid ground under feet just before the world re-solidified in front of her. "Where are we?"

"A world of our making."

"Ours?"

"Having someone magical in your life has it's perks. Like this." He watched her face.

Susan felt a sensual surge swell inside her. "Oh my."

He gave her a grin. "There's more where that came from."

Susan found her body naked, just like Warren's. "Oh show me more."

The End

A Fish Out of Water

Chapter One

"What the hell!" Sarah McIntyre's boss jumped up from the chair as hot coffee splashed into his crotch. "Damn it, Sarah! This is the third time this week. What has gotten into you?"

She wished she knew. Nerves, she guessed. "I don't know, Mr. Milici. Guess my mind was drifting."

Sarah shook her head to keep the tears from falling as she grabbed a napkin and started to blot at his crotch. She jumped when he grabbed the napkin from her hand.

"If you weren't so good at your job I would've fired you a long time ago." He dabbed the napkin against his suit. A quick look put a grimace on his face. "And get that coffeepot away from me."

"Yes, sir, and I'm sorry." Sarah sat the pot down on a filing cabinet. "It was an accident."

"I know. Why don't you take the rest of the afternoon off? Maybe you can pull yourself together? Find a date for the office function in a couple days?"

She nodded.

"And Sarah? One more screw up, and you won't be working here." He gestured at his clothes. "I can't afford the cleanup anymore."

Sarah slunk out of Mr. Milici's office and tried to ignore the snickers she heard coming from her co-workers. They were all jerks anyway.

Leaning her back against the door to the stairway, she pushed it open. It was five floors down, but she always took the stairs. Someone once asked her if she was afraid to take the elevator, and she laughed it off, but deep down inside she was. The last time she was on an elevator the darn thing wouldn't land on her floor, and she had to pull herself up out of the car onto her belly because the floor didn't come up high enough for her to just step out. Not very dignified in a two-piece suit.

Her car sat in the front row. The clank of her keys on the ground made her want to pound her head against the roof of her car, but she knew someone would be looking out the windows. Instead, she picked them up, unlocked her door and climbed inside.

A half hour later, she stood at the edge of the shore searching for rocks to throw. She really hated her life. Nothing worked in her favor. The job of her dreams turned out to be a nightmare—one of her own creation. She picked up a shell fragment. Anything to help focus her mind so she could figure out how to stop her klutziness.

"I wish…" She pitched one shell as hard as she could. "That I could find…" The second partial shell went flying. "A man. Wait. Not just any man." One of the fragments she held in her hand caught her eye. "Oh, this one is pretty. It's a keeper."

"Now let's see. Where was I?" She unconsciously rubbed the iridescent shell. "Right. I need a man who cares. Who will not judge me by my mistakes and quirks. Who has a big heart. Who will be willing to help me with my little problem without questions."

She spotted a partial conch shell. Finally, something with a little weight to it. A grin spread across her lips when she grabbed it. "This will make me feel better."

Like a baseball pitcher, she wound her arm up and let the shell fly.

A deep cry of pain fractured the air.

"What the…" She headed toward a cluster of boulders. "I didn't even throw in that direction."

Another sound filled the air. Sarah wasn't sure if she heard a growl this time or another wounded sound, but she definitely heard sounds of struggling. She darted between several boulders and found a man with his feet trapped. "You okay?"

He just stared at her.

"Do you need help getting up?" It looked like his feet were wedged between two rocks. She frowned when she noticed his bare feet. Glancing up his leg, she found no pants. "Holy cow!"

"Problem?" His voice came out rough, grainy. Like he had sand in his throat or had swallowed a lot of saltwater.

"Um, you—you're naked." She didn't mean to blurt it out but couldn't stop the words once she started talking. "I don't see too many naked men in public."

"Naked?" He stared at her with the most startling blue eyes.

Sarah noticed his voice seemed stronger. "Yeah, lack of clothing?" A moment ago she would have bolted from him, but something told her he needed her help.

"Oh."

The one word responses started to bother her. Didn't he have anything else to say? "Look. I don't mean to put you out."

"Put me out?" He paused for a moment. "Um. Is naked a bad thing?"

She blinked at his question. "Well, yeah, in public. Unless you want to go to jail without a stitch on." She couldn't help but like the view. He didn't seem to be shy about it either.

"No?"

"You don't sound convinced." She looked around to see if anyone was close enough to see him if he stood up. "If we're careful, I can get you to my car without you being seen."

"That's good?"

"Unless you want to be found here naked and trapped. This is the most popular beach in the area."

"And where are we?" He glanced up and down the beach like she did.

"Near Boston. Come on, we don't have much time." She stepped around him to get a good look at his feet. "How the heck did you do this? You're really wedged in."

He didn't answer. Just pushed and pulled against the rocks trapping him. A slight groan filled the air, and the rocks shifted enough to release his feet.

Sarah sucked in her breath when he stood up. *My god.* He stood about six foot four. Tall, thin. Nope, thin didn't work because his well-muscled body would never be called thin or skinny. Not bulky like the boys who flex their big biceps at the beach. He was more like a swimmer or a martial artist. Sleek. Yeah, that was the word, sleek. Like a porpoise or dolphin.

There was no way she would let him walk to her car like that. "Um, I might have a jacket or towel or something to cover you up in. Why don't you wait right here?"

"All right." He didn't sound that secure. "You promise to come back?"

"Sure do." She trudged through the sand in her bare feet. "What am I doing? He's naked. A total stranger. Could be some sort of masher."

Yet she kept walking. "I can't possibly be thinking of bringing this man home with me. All I need to do is just climb in my car and leave. At least that would be smart."

~ * ~

Mika watched as the sad young woman walked away. He sensed her anger and fear. There was something about her that drew him to her. He had only wanted to watch the humans play on the shore, not get trapped on land. But her inner song called to him. And now she was thinking about leaving him high and dry. Mika snorted at the thought before clearing his mind and sending his thoughts to her. *You don't want to leave this man alone. He needs you. You need him. He won't hurt you, and you know that.*

Her thoughts told him her name was Sarah. He watched as she paused by her car. Her mind jumbled as his thoughts mixed with hers. She was fighting him. Sarah feared him and the idea of befriending this stranger.

He felt sorry for her. She really had no choice now. Her heavy heart called him to the shore, and the shell she wished on made him answer her cry. The worst part was she didn't know it was all her doing and probably wouldn't understand if she did. *Humans. They can be so dense at times.*

A grin flitted across his face for a moment when he saw her walking back toward him with something in her hand. Good. She bowed under the pressure.

~ * ~

Sarah didn't know why she was walking back toward the stranger.

156

She didn't care how buff he looked, it was too dangerous, yet she couldn't seem to stop herself. "If I end up on the eleven o'clock news tonight, I'm going to kill myself." Of course, if she ended up on the news she'd most likely already be dead.

As she drew closer, she noticed his mouth. Was he trying to smile? His bared teeth looked more like he was getting ready to brush. Then it disappeared just as fast.

Her heart beat faster as she neared. Maybe she could give him the clothes and then leave. That would work. Be a Good Samaritan and then scram.

"Are those for me?" His pale blue eyes flashed in the sunlight.

All she could do was nod. He kept taking her breath away. How could a man be so good looking? Da Vinci could have used him as a model. In fact, every time she looked at him she kept thinking of *David*, the famous sculpture.

The clothes slipped through her fingers as he gently grasped them. They never broke eye contact as he slipped one arm and then another in the sleeves. A giggle escaped her when she realized he had the darn thing on backward. "If you keep wearing it that way you'll have problems breathing."

"Oh?" He took the garment off and looked at it like he didn't know what to do with it so she mimicked the procedure on how to put the jacket on. He gave her another strange smile as he slipped it on the right way.

Good thing it was an oversized sweat jacket. If it had been one of her suit jackets, the sleeves would have hit him about mid forearm, if he could get his arms in the sleeves. His smooth rippling chest would overpower the rest of the jacket. He'd look like a monkey. A handsome hairless one, but he would have looked ridiculous. That was for sure.

"Wrap this around your waist." She handed him a towel before pretending to wrap something around her.

He planted his hands on his hips. "What am I to do?"

Great, now she saw him as a pirate. "Wrap the towel around your waist to cover your—your—you know."

He looked down. A quick shrug and he wound the towel around his midsection.

"Come on." She turned her back on him and started to her car once more, hoping he wouldn't follow her.

A thud stopped her in her tracks. When she turned around, she didn't spot him. Not right away. It was his flailing feet in her peripheral vision that caught her eye. "What the—? What happened?"

"I'm not sure."

She helped him to his feet. "There's nothing to trip over."

"I'm sorry." He clung to her arm like a child. She couldn't help but notice he wasn't too sure on his feet. Was he drunk? That would explain so much! "Look, how about I drop you off at one of the missions. I'm sure they can help you dry out."

He stopped short at her words.

~ * ~

Dry out? No wonder humans were so crazy. If he dried out, he'd die. "I'll always need water."

She looked at him oddly.

What did he do wrong? *Don't humans drink water anymore?*

"Okay." She stopped in front of the metal box again. "I'll take you to the mission not too far from my work."

Sarah signaled him to walk around to the other side. Once she ducked her head and climbed inside he knew to follow suit, but climbing into that metal trap didn't sit well with him. It couldn't be safe. Mika lowered his head and crammed his large body into the small seat. A loud bang filled his head before it blasted with pain. He grabbed his head. A squeal escaped him.

"Oh, man that must have hurt."

He couldn't even nod, it hurt so bad. Closing his eyes, he hoped the pain would pass quickly. The warmth of Sarah's hand against his head surprised him. He jerked back. Except he hadn't gotten into the seat properly and his head was still too high. He banged it again. This time he leaned it forward and rested it on the hard form in front of him.

This thing was dangerous. A roar made him jump. This time with his hands on his head. The box vibrated.

"Put on your seatbelt."

What was that? He looked around and found a weird piece of cloth hanging from the ceiling of the vibrating box. Looking at Sarah, he noticed the thing coming across her chest and waist only to disappear beside the chair she sat in. Mika grabbed the material and found it pulled down easily, but he had no clue how to keep it from going back up into the ceiling.

She gave him a disgusted look before snatching the thing and jamming it into a small metal bracket he hadn't noticed before. A loud snap echoed in the car.

Mika stared forward. Not knowing what was going to happen next petrified him. The box vibrated harder as it slowly moved. "What are you doing?"

"Driving." She looked ahead of them, watching something, but kept glancing back at him. "Oh, come on. You can't tell me you've never been in a car before."

"Okay." He'd seen enough of these things from the edge of the ocean to know humans used them everywhere. They even drove on the sand in some places. But how would Sarah take it if he told her this was the first time he'd been on land. That he still hadn't quite gotten his earth legs yet. "I've never been in this type of car before."

The comment seemed to make her angrier. "I'm sorry if my little car doesn't live up to your standards, but then again I wasn't the one trapped, naked at the shore."

"I—watch out!" They veered around a corner surrounded by dry decaying dwellings. Humans were ninety-six percent water, just like his people. How could they survive like this?

"What? Are you from Europe?"

"Yes?" He wasn't sure what difference it made, but it placated her.

"Well then, hang on to your seat. This will only take a second."

He did as she asked and was grateful when she flew around another corner. Mika wasn't sure he could handle much more of this.

"Here we are." The box slowed down and stopped in front of one of the dry dwellings. A big wooden sign hung over the door claiming anyone could enter. The largest letters stated it was the South Street Mission. "This is where you can stay."

She wasn't getting out of the car. What did he need to do to stay with her? "I can't go in there."

"You have to." Sarah turned in her seat to stare at him. A hint of fear filled her eyes.

He didn't like knowing he put that look there. "It doesn't smell very good." The odor floating out the doors wrinkled his nose and churned his stomach. He didn't think he could go in there without becoming ill.

Sarah turned toward the door. Her hair had a thousand highlights in the sun. So beautiful.

"I'm not going to hurt you." Her emotions lay so close to the surface he could read them easily. "I promise."

She turned back to look at him. Sunlight danced in her eyes. "You don't understand."

"I do." Mika looked deep in her eyes. Her heart would accept the truth. "You're afraid I'm some sort of crazy guy that will do great harm to you. I'm not that sort of man."

"And how do I know I can trust you?" She slapped her hand over her mouth the moment the words slipped out.

He took her hand and placed it on his heart. "I'm here to protect you. To help you."

"Help me?" She pulled her hand away. "Who said I needed help?"

"You did."

"I did not." She inched back in her seat.

"You did." He leaned forward and touched her heart. "In here."

"You're crazy." Sarah scrambled out of her car. "I don't know who you are, where you came from. I want you out of my car and out of my life."

Now what? He had to convince her to keep him. If he didn't, he would never go home.

Chapter Two

She stood on the concrete looking lost and sad. It came off her in waves. In fact, it was attracting the wrong type of people. Several slimy men surrounded her.

"Hey, sister, you looking for a good time?" One of them stepped close to her, making her body tense.

Mika didn't think. In seconds, he had stepped out of the car and put himself between her and the foul smelling man. "You will not harm the lady."

"And who are you? Her guardian angel?"

"Her protector." He stared down at the other man.

"I ain't gonna hurt her, just want to talk to her." He smiled when he noticed what Mika had on. "Lost your clothes?"

"It was destroyed when I proved to another man that I was her protector."

"You talk funny, dude."

Mika stopped for a moment and opened his mind to the thoughts of those around him. Thousands of voices filled his head, different languages, colloquiums, phrases. "Forget how funny I talk and understand that I'll break every bone in your body if you step any closer." He grabbed the man by his collar and lifted him off the ground. A quick shake followed to show he was serious. Just to make sure the other man got his message, Mika puffed up his chest.

The man gave him a weird look but nodded. When Mika put his feet back on the ground, the guy took a step back.

Someone tugged on his arm. It was Sarah.

"Get in the car," she said in a soft voice.

Car. Now he knew what to call the box. "But—"

"Now." She pulled a little harder. "Before the rest of those guys put their minds together and beat the crap out of you." She kept tugging on his arm, forcing his feet to move.

"But I don't want to get back in that thing."

"You have to." Sarah looked up at him with frightened eyes. "I don't think I can handle the thought of you being hurt after the way you stood up for me. If we don't get out of here you will be."

He nodded and headed to his side. Mika tugged on the door, but it wouldn't budge. His fingers wrapped around the handle, and he felt something slide in under his finger. Another pull opened the door.

He climbed in, making sure he didn't hit his head. The little piece of cloth slid easily over him to snap in the metal snap next to his hip. The car started to vibrate, which made him grip the material in front of him.

"I promise it will be okay, but I need to get us out of here." The vibration picked up as the car moved faster.

"Please make this stop soon!"

"Stop being such a baby." Sarah flicked her hair behind her ear. "My house is a couple of blocks away."

The car took a few more curves before it slowed down, took one more turn, and stopped moving. He exhaled deeply. They made it.

Sarah stood on the concrete before he realized she had climbed out. "Well come on, before I regret this."

"You won't." He gave her his best smile as he stepped out of the car. She covered a small laugh and headed toward one of the dwellings he hated.

"I'm not holding this door forever." She commented when he stood, staring at the building instead of following her inside.

"Sorry." He took a deep breath and started moving. The closer he got to the glass door, the slower he moved. This couldn't be good. The decaying smell of rotten earth alone kept him from entering. Sarah didn't seem to be bothered by it. "So. This is where you live?"

She spoke, but he didn't hear a word because he found the ground suddenly rushing up to his face.

~ * ~

162

Sarah stared dumbfounded as her knight in shining armor took a dive. How graceful can he be? And what did he trip over? The doorframe? Grabbing his arm, she pulled him to his feet and propelled him to the elevator. He started to really fight her when he realized they were headed for the double doors. At that point, she didn't care if he had a phobia against small spaces. They only had to go up four flights. She could handle him for that long. Why she wanted to, she wasn't real sure, but getting him into her apartment was her goal, and nothing was going to stop her.

Her biggest hope was no one saw them together. All she needed was one of her nosy neighbors talking about her bringing some strange man home. Why was she doing this anyway? Each time she tried to leave him behind, she found she couldn't. Sarah didn't know what was going on, but she was feeling a bit manipulated. Still she did need a date for her work function, and he was the only man who didn't know about her klutziness. Would he be willing to go?

He walked around her apartment looking at everything. His fingers slid along the edge of the different surfaces. Facial expressions followed. Every surface was different, and he absorbed them all. There were a couple of times when he went back to touch a fabric or surface. Like he had never felt them before.

Maybe asking him wasn't a good idea.

Here she went again, questioning her own actions. Yet each time she ignored her own council. What was wrong with her?

~ * ~

Mika could see she was starting to second-guess what she was doing again. Time for him to get to the heart of the matter. On the table sat a beautiful envelope. He had seen it in her mind enough to know that was why she wished for him in the first place. "What is this?"

"Oh nothing. Just an invitation." She picked up the thick envelope and ran her fingers over it.

"Oh." This was it. All he had to do is ask the right questions. "Can I ask where to?"

"It's a business function. Nothing major." She scuffed her foot against the soft floor before speaking again. "Um. Are you doing anything in a couple of days? Saturday evening?"

He had no idea what day that was. "Being with you?"

"You're very sweet. I, ah, I need a date." Her voice cracked, making her feel like a schoolgirl. After clearing it, she started over. "Ahem, I need a date for my work function. It's this Saturday. Will you go with me?"

"Of course." He gave her his best smile. A squared mouth with nothing but teeth.

"Have you seen that thing in the mirror? You're going to frighten small children." She grabbed his hand and dragged him, something she did a lot with this man, to the big mirror hanging in the hallway. "Now smile."

He bared his teeth.

"See? You look like some sort of masher. Relax, just smile."

"But I am."

"Look at the difference between our smiles." Why was she doing this? How much more could she antagonize this guy? Was this her way of driving him away? It didn't seem to be working.

He turned his head this way and that, looking at his mouth then hers. His fingers glided across her jaw to outline the seam of her lips, of her smile. It sent chills through her body and made her nervous. Made her think of things she shouldn't. Want things she shouldn't.

"Um, what do I call you anyway?" The jitters had her stepping away and heading to the mail sitting on the floor by the door. Anything to keep her hands occupied.

"Mika."

"Meeka," she sounded out. At least she had a name to go with the face. *Stop it. You need a date, not a lot of trouble.*

"What do I need to do this date thing?"

Date thing? Oh yeah, you picked a good one, girl. She smiled. "A suit would be nice."

"Suit." He nodded. "What's a suit?"

"Oh good Lord." She snagged his hand once more and pulled him to the computer in her bed room. She didn't know why he kept acting like he had no clue what she was talking about, but she'd play along for a little while longer. "This is my computer." She tapped a few keys. "This is the world wide web. Meet Google dot com. Any question you have they should be able to answer."

She turned her back and headed for the door. She could hear him grumbling but didn't know what he said. "Spelling out words on the key pads will help."

~ * ~

Mika stared at the weird little box with the picture on it. It showed so much. "So what do I do now?"

He turned to look at the doorway Sarah had just walked through. He didn't like reading her mind so much, but it was the only way he would learn how to run this computer. Clearing his thoughts, he connected with her, only looking for how to run the machine in front of him. "Interesting."

He flexed his fingers and typed a few words in the slot to start his search. First, he had to see what was expected for someone to wear to a business function. Whatever that was. It took a few searches before he hit on the right page to show him what one would wear on a date. Someone named Levi showed him what was worn on a casual date. He then searched for business clothing. "Now I have to figure out how to merge the look."

Maybe he needed a little more information. He came out into the hall just as a loud shrilling noise filled the room. His body slammed against the wall.

"Hello?" asked Sarah. "Oh, hi. Yeah. Today was pretty bad. Oh my God! It was so embarrassing. I spilled coffee all over him, and then I tried to blot it off his crotch. I don't know what possessed me to do that. I know. Can you imagine? What? Oh that. I do. No. I'm not sure if he's the smartest choice, but I'm sort of limited now, aren't I?"

Who was she talking to? She held a small silver bar to her ear and continued to chatter away.

He stepped into the room she paced in, and she turned toward him.

"Look, I have to go." She snapped the silver bar in half then stuffed it in her pocket. "You need some help?"

"I had a quick question." She was still questioning her choice in him. He had to fix it some how. "How business is this dinner?"

Barbara Donlon Bradley

"Suit and tie. Nothing too fancy."

He saw those on the web sites earlier. It shouldn't be too difficult, and it sure would be better than the towel and sweat jacket he still had on.

"We do need something better for you to wear. Where is your bank?"

He gave her a blank look. Did it mean the same thing above water as it did underwater? "It's a long distance away."

"Don't they have an office nearby?"

"No." He hoped that would make her happy.

"What? You still with a small mom and pop bank?" She put her hands on her hips.

"Yes." He didn't know what else to say.

"How far is it?"

Further than she could go. "I can go by myself."

"I can drive."

How was he going to get out of this one? First, he needed to be sure they were talking about the same thing. "I'm very protective of my account. I'd rather do this alone. Um, how much do I need?"

"I'm not sure how much a suit would cost. Couple hundred?"

Good, it was money, but what was a hundred? Maybe his father would know. "It won't take me long." What was the phrase he had heard at the shore many times? "See you later."

He walked out the door before Sarah could stop him. It shouldn't take him long to get to the sea. They didn't drive far. Although he didn't know his way around the area, his nose led him to the ocean right away.

Making sure no one watched, he stripped off the sweatshirt and towel. He was grateful for his ability to mask himself when around humans. It didn't last long but got him from her apartment to here without someone realizing he was pretty much naked. One more look and he slipped into his medium. He loved the feel of water surrounding his body. He had missed it so much the last few hours.

Water slid around his body as he descended deeper. A couple of flips along the way put a smile on his face, but it slipped away the moment he saw his home. No one believed in Atlantis. No human, anyway. Yet, here it was in all its glory.

Humans believed several fantastic tales, but none were right. His favorite was the cataclysmic disaster that caused the island to sink. The island never sank. It was always underwater. There was a time when his people could walk freely amongst humans. When Atlantians had nothing to fear. When a merman could slip in and out of the water without anyone thinking twice about it. A sigh escaped him.

Now his people were nothing more than a myth. In order for them to interact with humans, they had to become one.

"Sick of the air breathers already?"

Mika spun at the sound of his father's voice. "We're air breathers when we want to be."

His father laughed. "True, but humans can't breathe in water the way we can. Turns them a little blue. So, what brought you back so soon? Did the girl kick you out?"

"No." Mika realized he should have paid more attention to his father's words. He sounded just like Sarah. "And how often do you spy on them? You sound just like the people I've been talking to the last few hours."

"Enough." His father swam around him. "Hmmm You're here because…" His father stroked his beard. "You want to impress her! You like this human!"

"She's okay." He wasn't about to tell his dad anything about Sarah. With his luck, he'd want to join him on land. "She's asked me to be her date."

"Really? Then you need money, unless you want to check the chests at home for clothing."

"And run the risk that I end up with a suit from the Bronze Age? No thank you. Since you know what money is, maybe you can explain it to me?"

"It's the way their entire world works. So many of them don't do physical labor anymore. Most trading has become obsolete. Except for trading their currency in for product. It's a little confusing if you've never used it." His father floated beside him. "But it's easy to learn."

"And you're willing to teach me? What's the catch?" Mika questioned his father's offer. As much as he loved the man, he had to be wary of the man's practical jokes.

"No catch." He placed his hand on his chest. "Promise."

"Dad. I remember your last promise. I swam into ninth grade with purple hair."

"Well, it was big with the humans." His father slapped him on the back. "You know I have always been fascinated by the earth dwellers."

"Dad."

"Okay, okay. So I've watched too many movies. Sue me."

Mika rolled his eyes. "Dad. Please behave."

"Fine. You can use any of the gold. We have no use for it here. Every time I go topside it grows in value. I'd love to know how much it's worth now."

"Thanks, Dad. I owe you."

"Does that mean I can come back with you?"

"No."

Chapter Three

He tugged on his waistband before he knocked on Sarah's door. These pants were very uncomfortable. Binding. And why did they put such a dangerous contraption so close to such a delicate part of the body.

Sarah opened the door and just stared at him. "May I help you?"

"Sarah? I'm Mika, remember?"

"Mika? Good grief! I didn't recognize you in clothes." She slapped her hand over her mouth and looked around. "That didn't sound very good, did it? Come in."

He stepped past her as she moved to the side to let him in. He heard the door close once he was in her living room. "Is this okay?"

She looked him up and down, walking slowly in a circle around him. "It'll do."

~ * ~

Sarah found herself on the verge of drooling. *Goodness, doesn't he clean up nice.* She didn't even recognize him when he knocked on the door. His shoulders looked broader, his legs longer. She had seen him naked and found him more appealing in clothing, wondering when she might get a glimpse of that wonderful physique hiding underneath again.

What's wrong with me? She cleared her throat. "That's a nice outfit, but you'll need something a little dressier for the work function."

"I think I have that covered. Would you like to see?" He looked hopeful.

She gave a quick frown before nodding. "If it will make you feel better then sure."

He grinned and darted into the bathroom.

Sarah went back in the kitchen to wipe down the counters. Once she finished, all she had to do was mop the floor. It wasn't something she liked doing, but she hated bugs even more. The busy work kept her mind off the man in the other room.

At least for a few minutes.

Now her thoughts flew right back where she didn't want them. Had Mika changed his pants yet? Or was he just sliding them down his muscular legs? Did he have an unbuttoned shirt draped over his shoulders with his bare chest exposed?

"Okay. Okay. Okay." She flopped her hands around as she stomped her feet. "Need to get my thoughts on something else. Anything else. Bugs Bunny, Bugs Bunny. Bugs Bunny." She leaned her hands against the counter and closed her eyes to block out anything that could distract her.

"What are you doing?"

Her eyes popped open, and she straightened at Mika's words. "Oh. Just clearing my thoughts."

"Okay." He held out his arms. "What do you think?"

"Wow." He wore a simple black blazer over black Docker pants. The soft coral shirt added to the simple yet elegant look.

"I'm not sure what to do with this thing." Mika held up a tie.

"Stick that in your pocket. I don't think you need it." Sarah leaned her back against the counter and drank in the view. How lucky could she be? He was going to be her date for the party.

Mika liked the look in Sarah's eyes. All soft and gleaming. He caught a whiff of something. Her. She liked what she saw and was sending him a silent message. His own instinct kicked in. Sliding closer to her, he inhaled deeply. "So this will be okay for your function?"

Sarah nodded and looked up into his eyes. They were beautiful. She could get lost in them. The color of the ocean on a sunny day. As he watched her, his eyes darkened to a deeper blue green.

A soft scent wrapped around her, a salty fresh scent that made her think of the beach. What was it about him? It couldn't be because that was where she found him. She had met other men there, but they never smelled this clean. In fact, she didn't want to think about what they smelled like because some of them were pretty bad.

Mika's hand caressed her cheek before sliding into her hair. "So soft."

Sarah sighed at his words. His touch was as soft as silk. She felt like she was the most precious thing on the planet when he touched her like that. The heat from his body enveloped her. His fingers worked magic in her hair as they slipped in deep and massaged her scalp.

A soft moan escaped her as she tilted her head back to enjoy the massage. Heat seared her as Mika's lips pressed against her throat. The soft pressure sent chills down her spine. His arms slipped around her waist, pulling her into his body. Wherever their bodies touched, fire burned her. All along her thighs and hips. Her breasts pressing against his chest took her breath away. She could feel every intake of breath, every muscle tighten and loosen as he tightened his grip.

Mika's lips opened slightly, and her knees went weak. His tongue slid along the seam of her lips, begging for entrance. Soft. Hard. Sensuous. She opened her mouth and felt his tongue invade hers. It slid along her teeth and gums, searching for something. She didn't know what he was looking for, but she prayed he wouldn't find it quickly.

Their tongues twined together. Doing a dance as old as time. Warmth furled within her. Flames licked along her skin. Her heart pounded in her chest.

~ * ~

Mika felt her body flush as desire raced through her blood. She was so sexual, he could feel every emotion she felt. He knew what nibbled away at that desire. It wouldn't take much to make her his. But he needed her to take control. She had to really want it, and as much as her body told him not to stop, Sarah's mind was rebelling.

He withdrew his tongue and placed soft butterfly kisses all along her collarbone before trailing them along her jaw line. Resting his forehead against hers, he willed his heart to slow down. Every nerve screamed for release. "You taste so good."

Her body melted against him a little more. Much more and he wouldn't know where he ended and where she started.

"I need to…" What word did he need? He needed water, either to drink or to surround his body, "…cool off."

"A shower might help." Her voice raspy.

He smiled. He did that to her. "That sounds good."

She took his hand and led him down the hall to the bathroom. The small room smelled of water. His whole body reacted to it. Sarah felt his reaction and gave him a sultry look before leaving the room. If he wasn't afraid of her reaction to his unique difference to humans, he'd drag her into the shower and finish what he started.

Turning the knobs on the sink as an experiment let him know how to get the water out. C meant cold and H had to be hot. He turned toward the tub and wondered how to block the water from running down the drain. He didn't see anything to use so he sat on the lip of the tub and stared. There was a spout up above his head. Had they created a waterfall? What fun!

He stripped his clothes off and turned on the cold water. It streamed down out of the overhead spout. Mika stepped in and tilted his head up toward the water. It felt wonderful.

As the water saturated his skin, he felt the change come over him. "Oh no."

~ * ~

A load plop then a splash came out of the bathroom. Oh crap, did he fall? "Mika? You all right?"

His voice floated through the wall. "Everything is fine, just fine. No problem here."

She could hear him scrambling around. "I'm coming in."

Mika was draping his arms over the top of the tub when she walked in. How weird. He had the shower on yet sat in the tub. What was worse, he had one of her good towels draped across his legs, the one with the silky material and the little roses embroidered on it. "Um, I can get you a better towel."

"No. No. This is fine." He straightened the towel so it completely covered the bottom half of his body.

"It's no problem." She grabbed the towel and tugged. Mika tugged right back. A strong odor of fish filled the air. *Where the hell did that come from?* "I can get you a bigger towel."

"That would be great."

But he wouldn't relinquish the one he clutched to his body. Most men would be flaunting what nature gave them, and she had felt that nice gift when they kissed earlier. He had nothing to be ashamed of.

A sigh escaped her as she let go of the towel and snagged another from the shelves she had mounted on the wall. She placed the towel on the closed toilet lid and backed out. "Whenever you're ready to climb out of there."

~ * ~

Mika slumped against the tub. That was too close. He whipped the soaked towel off his legs to reveal a tail fin. The moment the water hit his legs they reverted to a tail, and he couldn't stand on a tail. He went down like a ton of kelp.

Sarah came running and he grabbed the first thing he could get his hands on. Lucky the towel was long enough to cover all of him. He didn't think it would have been a good thing for her to see a fin sticking out of it. Mika had to bend part of his tail to keep it out of sight. It hurt, but he couldn't imagine her reaction if he hadn't. It probably would have gone over like a mackerel flopping in a fry pan.

He struggled to get his body out of the tub. Once he flopped to the floor, he used the towel to rub the water off his legs. The change took some time, but soon he had two appendages instead of one big one. He wondered if any contact with water would do this. The small seat with water had him thinking. Mika stuck a hand into the water to see what would happen. Nothing.

So what would happen if he stuck a foot in it? Scales showed up immediately. "Okay so contact to water on the lower half is a no-no."

"Who are you talking to?"

Sarah's voice made him jump. Was she eavesdropping? "Myself." No one else was there to hear him.

"I've made coffee if you'd like some." Her footsteps faded as she walked back toward the kitchen.

So she had a reason for being there. Or was that just a quick excuse? He'd been hanging around humans too much. He was just as paranoid as they were. He finished drying off and climbed back into his clothes. A heavy aroma filtered through his nose, drawing him out of the bathroom and into the area where Sarah sat.

She clutched a cup to her face. Steam rose off the dark liquid. She inhaled deeply before taking a drink.

What was it about the liquid that made her react that way? He had to find out.

"Want some?"

"Sure." He had no clue what he was asking for, but he had to see what had made her mellow out and calm down.

Sarah stood and poured him a cup of the dark liquid. "Cream or sugar?"

He didn't know, so he shrugged.

She did the same and went to the refrigerator. "I have both so I'll set them out for you okay?"

Mika nodded and sat in a chair next to the table where she placed the cup. A quick sniff made him smile. It smelled wonderful. He put the cup to his lips and took a small sip. The bitter brew made his face pinch up.

"Oh good heavens, put some cream and sugar in it. I won't think you less a man if you do." She grabbed a small glass bottle and poured a white liquid into his cup. The two swirled together and created a lighter brown.

He took another sip and found the bitter taste had disappeared. This he could drink. Sarah sat back in her chair and cupped her mug. Mika mimicked her movements.

"The function isn't until tomorrow evening. Do you have a place to stay?"

She was back to that again. "No. I live a great distance from here. I can go home but I can't be sure I'll be back in time for tomorrow evening."

Her face sank at his words. "Oh."

He wanted to ask if he could stay but felt she just might tell him no if he asked now. She had to come to this decision on her own. No glamour this time either.

~ * ~

How the heck was she supposed to keep him underfoot for another twenty-four hours? He hadn't been in her apartment more than an hour, and he kissed her so well she nearly melted. What would happen if they were together for a night? Her mind boggled over what her imagination started dreaming up.

He sat there so innocently watching her, clutching a cup of something she knew he had never had before. His face gave him away.

There was so much about him that didn't make sense. There was no way he had ever set foot in a car. Not by the way he gripped the dashboard. He didn't even know how to use the seatbelt. Yet, he leaped out of the car when she needed him most. Without thought over what would happen to him. A knight in shining armor. How could she deny him anything when he did that?

She turned her back to him. *What to do, what to do? He needs me.* Sarah was sure of that. But was it safe? She waffled back and forth for a few minutes before she finally came to a decision. When she turned back toward Mika, he still watched her with the cup clutched in his hands.

"I guess it would be okay if you stay here for the time being, but you'll have to sleep on the couch."

He smiled. Mika was getting that down. It lit up his face and put a special glow in his eyes. "I promise you won't regret it."

She might, but as long as they had some ground rules, everything would be fine. "We need to get a few things clear first."

"Like what?' He took another sip. "You know, this isn't too bad."

"I know." Why did he have to distract her like that? "I have extra pillows and blankets."

"Okay."

He looked around but never noticed the pillows and blankets. What was his deal? "And I can't sleep with the TV on so you'll have to do without."

"Fine." He didn't seem to be bothered by that.

"I'm a morning person."

"Hey. Me too." Mika was all excited because they both loved mornings. "I don't think I've missed a sunrise in years. Can I see the sun from here?"

Crap. "Um, I don't know." She flapped her arms around. "Most of the time the sun is up by the time I'm ready for work."

"Ah."

Now she was embarrassed. "Anyway, we can order in then watch a little TV, but I go to bed pretty early."

"Okay."

Just how dense was he? "By myself."

He nodded.

"Without you."

"Right. What's a TV?"

She growled and hit the button on the remote. Mika jumped three feet when sound blared from the speakers. He then stared at the screen like a child seeing his favorite toy in the window of a department store.

"I've never seen anything like this!" He sat in front of the screen and watched in rapt attention. After a moment or two, he got up and touched the screen and the back of the TV. "How do they fit the people in the box?"

"It's a transmission."

"A what?" That caught his attention for a minute. Then he turned into a typical man, sitting down again and staring at the screen.

She sighed and plopped on the couch next to him. So, he wasn't that different after all.

"A transmission, huh? How does it work?" He jumped up again and dashed to the television.

"Um, I wouldn't touch—" A blue spark arched from the TV to Mika's fingers. He yelped and jumped up on the sofa. "That hurt!"

"Get down." She tried to keep her face straight as she answered. "Static electricity will do that to you."

"What's static electricity?"

Sarah didn't know how to explain it. "It's just something that happens when the environment is a little too dry." He put his hands on his hips in an 'I told you so' manner. "What?"

"Nothing." He dropped his hands and climbed off the couch to sit again. "So what does this box do?"

"The television? Same basic stuff any other TV shows." She picked up the remote and clicked a button. The screen changed to a cartoon.

Mika leaped back up on the couch. "What is that?" He leaned

forward with wide eyes. Grabbing the remote from her, Mika proceeded to flip through the channels quickly. "Wow!"

"Get down." Mika was like a puppy. Except if he kept jumping up on the couch all the time she'd have to replace her sofa.

He ignored her, squealing when he found something he found fascinating. What had she created? When Mika found the volume button, she had to cover her ears so she could handle noise. "That's a bit loud."

"What?" He grinned at her like a child.

She snagged the remote and lowered the volume. "This is to control the volume, not blow eardrums."

"Sorry." He took the remote back and continued to click away. He paused from time to time. Either to look at a colorful commercial or hear a catchy tune. Pretty girls also made him pause. Something that seemed to irk her.

"Pick a channel and stick with it."

"How can you make a choice when there is so much to choose from?" Mika handed over the remote.

"My goodness, if you watched TV every night like the rest of the world you'd be complaining there was nothing on." She chose an old movie for them to watch. Something they wouldn't have to pay attention to if they started to talk. Darryl Hannah and Tom Hanks popped up on the screen.

Mika stared at the screen as the two actors interacted. The scene was in a restaurant. Darryl bit into the lobster, surprising Tom and all the extras in the scene.

"Oh this is such a cute movie. She's a mermaid."

"Really? People believe in mermaids?" He sounded hopeful.

"They're mythological creatures. Sure, there are some people who believe in them but overall? They fall into the realm of faeries and leprechauns. We want to believe, but there's no evidence."

"So." He turned and placed an arm on the back of the sofa. "You would believe in these things if you had proof?"

"I don't know. I mean, I guess."

Chapter Four

Mika thought for a moment. All he had to do was show he was a 'mermaid' as the humans called them, and she'd have to believe. The fins were pretty hard to ignore. Then maybe she'd believe he was there because of her.

But was she ready to be confronted with the truth? He didn't think so.

"Is pizza okay?" Sarah picked up another small box. It was the little silver one she snapped in half earlier. She opened it up and pushed against the inside. "Hello? Yes. I'd like the regular. Make that two. What? Yes. Twenty minutes. Great. Thanks."

Mika snatched the box before she could close it. "And what is this?"

"A phone." She pulled it from his grasp and closed it. "Don't tell me you've never seen a phone before."

He blinked at her. "Not one like that." At least he wasn't lying. Mika wanted a better look at it but didn't want to anger her. Maybe he'd get a better look later.

"It's a typical flip phone." She placed it on the small table beside the couch. As long as she didn't put it in her pocket like she did the last time he might be able to study it.

Coffee, TV, flip phones. No wonder his father liked to disappear for days at a time. He couldn't wait for this pizza thing. He had heard many humans talk about it. Now he was going to experience it first hand. Wouldn't his father be proud.

It didn't take long before he heard another noise that made him jump. Sarah headed to the door like she knew what made it. She pressed a box on the wall. This world sure had a lot of boxes. He wondered why humans were so fascinated with them.

"Yes?" she said.

"Frankie's Pizza."

"Right. I'll be right down. She slipped out the door, leaving him alone. The first thing he grabbed was the phone. The face lit up when he opened it. It also started to make noise, and he slapped it shut again. Mika was glad he did because the moment he sat it on the table Sarah came back into the room.

"Dinnertime." She sailed back in the door carrying two thin boxes. Again with the boxes. The heady aroma coming from the boxes made his mouth water. A loud growl filled the air.

Sarah laughed. "Come on." She placed the box on a table then went into the other room for a moment before returning with some paper products. "Well, flip the lid."

Okay. What was a lid? He looked at the box and noticed a seam. Pulling on it, the top popped up easily, revealing an ugly circular thing. At least it wasn't a box.

Sarah pulled a piece of the circle apart and put it on something before handing it to him. "I'm assuming you've never had this before."

"What gave me away?"

"The horrified look on your face." She laughed again. It was a melodious sound that brightened his mood. "I promise it tastes a lot better than it looks. Just close your eyes." She picked up a piece and closed her eyes. "And take a bite."

He watched as ecstasy raced across her face. If it was that good, he couldn't wait to try it. Mika picked up his piece and closed his eyes. If he looked at it too long, he might not want to try it. Taking a deep breath, he asked Poseidon to watch over him and bit into the gooey red mess.

Flavor exploded in his mouth. Spices he had never had before bathed taste buds. "This is great." He muffled through a mouthful.

"Thought you'd like it." She handed him a square cloth then picked up another one for herself and wiped her face with it.

He nodded vigorously and stuffed the rest of the slice in his mouth. As he tried to chew, he realized he might have put too much in his mouth. He couldn't close it.

"Sorry." The words came out muffled again. It sounded more like 'forry'. It took a couple swallows before he got all of the food to slide down his throat.

Sarah sat opposite of him, keeping her eyes averted and taking only one bite before chewing and swallowing. There was so much to learn about humans. They even ate differently. Of course, their food didn't float in front of them whenever they wanted to eat.

Sarah ate another piece before moving to the couch and the TV. That thing was so fascinating. She had turned on a movie, as she called it, when he joined her. This one was also about strange creatures. At least to Sarah. He didn't have the heart to tell her many of the old legends were very real.

They sat on the couch and watched the TV for several hours before Sarah yawned and stretched.

"I'm going to get some sleep."

He nodded. What had she mentioned? Blanket and pillows. Sleeping in the air would be interesting. Sarah handed him a pile of fluff and bid him goodnight. Now what was he supposed to do with this?

Mika sat it on the floor and stretched out on the couch. He found he couldn't get comfortable so he picked up the fluffy white rectangle and put it under his head. Much better. He pulled on the other pile of fluff and found it unfolded. This he lay on top of him and found himself wrapped in a cocoon of warmth. It didn't take long before he dozed off.

In his dreams, he was home with his father. He reminded Mika of his obligation. "Don't fall in love with a human. Our people need you to come home. I've led them long enough. It's now your turn."

He then found himself trapped in a kelp farm. The long reeds wrapped around him, dragging him down. The more he fought, the tighter the tendrils wrapped around his arms and legs.

Suddenly he was free.

Wham!

"Ow!" Mika rubbed his head where it collided with the coffee table. He found himself on the floor with the blanket wrapped around him. So much for the kelp farm. He tugged free and walked to a window. Water ran down the clear exterior.

It was raining. As much as he wanted to go out into it, Mika didn't know how to get back in if he left the building. Sarah hadn't explained that to him.

The room suddenly lit up like it was daytime before it darkened again. Rolling noise followed.

Boom, boom, boom, *boom, boom*!

A whimper filled the air. Mika followed the sound until he came to a closed door. Should he go in? Bright light illuminated the hallway before another loud crack of thunder vibrated through the rooms. A high pitched scream shattered the quiet and filled him with dread.

~ * ~

Sarah sat bolt straight in her bed when the lightening flashed. That was too close. Her mind rebelled against the fear she kept in tight control. It burst through her consciousness, breaking through all the barriers she had built to stop it from surfacing. Terror, sharp and clear, raced through her. She snagged the doorknob and wrenched the door open. Without thinking or looking, she flung herself through the doorway and right into something hard.

Warm hands circled her arms. "Sarah?"

She couldn't talk. Her body shook uncontrollably.

"Sarah." Strong arms wrapped around her. Fire raced through her veins where their bodies touched. She fought against the bands holding her. "Relax, it's me."

The voice didn't register. She had to get away from the sound that wouldn't leave her alone. She'd do anything to get away from it. "Help me."

Mika smoothed his hands against her hair. "Why are you so frightened?"

"Can't stand the noise." She buried herself into his body.

He didn't know what she was doing, but it felt like heaven. She pressed tightly against him. Her velvet soft skin slid against his. Her arms brushed the hairs of his, causing goose bumps to rise. Her hair slipped over his shoulder where her head rested and caressed his back. Its silky texture caused him to suck in a breath. His body tightened as the tendrils danced across his nerves. Desire gripped him hard and fast.

Mika closed his eyes as he tried to control his need. He couldn't let

181

his base nature take control. Not when he swore to fulfill the wish she made that day on the beach.

Sarah placed little kisses all along his jaw. "Please. I need to forget the noise. At least for a little while."

"I can't take advantage of you." He tried to extricate himself from her embrace but found her grip tighter than an octopus'.

She wrapped her arms around him and jumped so she could throw her legs around his waist. He slammed against the wall with her weight. "You won't be taking advantage of me. I promise not to regret this in the morning."

"Sarah."

"Shut up, and kiss me." She locked lips with him as she rocked against him.

Mika lost control when she thrust her tongue into his mouth. Nothing mattered anymore. The only thing he could think of was the woman in his arms and how much he needed to be inside her.

He pushed her against the opposite wall as he took control of the kiss. He felt her smile against his lips. She thought she had the upper hand, but he knew it wouldn't last longer than thirty seconds.

He ran his tongue along her teeth, inhaling every breath she took. Mika broke the kiss to come up for air. His lips didn't remain still. They nipped her chin, nose, and right ear before he planted tiny butterfly kisses all along her jaw and neck. He forced a groan from her when he bit the skin on her collarbone and pulled it a little.

Sarah's skin heated up as he lathed his way down the dip between her breasts. Her skin had just the right amount of salt. It reminded him of the ocean. He loved the taste of it.

Her shirt buttoned down the front and opened easily to his questing fingers. Sarah pushed her head back against the wall when his fingers grazed her hot stomach. Mika needed to explore that as well but not from that angle. However, Sarah had other ideas. She gripped his butt and pulled him harder against her. That made him moan.

"We need to slow down," he murmured against her skin.

"No way." She bit his right ear. "I'm too hot for us to slow down. If you don't hurry, I think I'm going to go up in flames."

"Are you sure?"

She ripped his shirt apart. "Does that answer your question?"

He growled low in his throat. Mika tore her shirt off and threw it down the hallway. It took a moment to figure out how to release the drawstring that held the soft pants hugging her hips. A quick tug and they bagged against her. He found he now had easy access to any part of her body.

"We're not quite even yet." Her voice was soft and raspy against his throat.

"And how do you want to remedy that?" He brushed his lips against her temple.

"Take off your pants." It was her turn to bite him on the collarbone.

"What?" He couldn't think straight. Her lips kept him distracted.

She grabbed the top of his pants and pulled. The top button slipped free. She then forced the zipper down as far as she could before she hooked her fingers into the belt loops.

"You are very good at this," he ground out.

"First time, but desperate times call for desperate measures. Not bad, huh?" She had his pants down to his knees. Wrapping her fingers around him, she guided him to her, and using her heels, she pushed him inside her. He felt so good. Her muscles tightened instinctively.

Mika bit his lip to keep the moan deep in his throat from escaping. Her warm flesh tightened against him, surrounded him. He had never felt anything like it before. Physical joining between his people was nothing like this.

Sarah started to move against him, creating a rhythm and friction. His whole body shook with joy. His breath caught in his throat. No wonder humans enjoyed this so much.

His blood rushed through his veins. His skin was on fire. Flames of desire licked at his soul. Mika was grateful Sarah knew what she was doing because he was too caught up in the sensations. He followed her lead and picked up the pace when she did. He needed to taste her as he moved inside her. His lips connected with her skin. A slight salty taste raised his desire higher. He took control this time, moving in and out of Sarah with need. With every move, he stoked the fire. Sarah moaned in his arms. She sucked in her breath as her muscles tightened around him. Her body started to vibrate as her climax began. She locked her legs around him in a vise grip as she moved faster against him.

Gripping her hips, he started to move faster against her, pounding her against the wall. Sarah laughed. He needed more. His body tightened. His heart wanted to burst from his chest. The power of an orgasm forced a shout out of him. Sarah screamed right after him.

Mika watched Sarah's face in the afterglow of her climax. What now?

Chapter Five

Sarah rested her head against his shoulder as she drifted back to earth. Her mind cleared as well. Oh good grief, what had she done? It was the best sex she had ever had but not the smartest move she ever made.

Thunderstorms were her worst nightmare. "Um."

Mika still had his head thrown back. She could still feel the spasms race through him. Was it as good for him as it had been for her?

He sighed and opened his eyes. "That was amazing."

Sarah blushed a bright red. Her legs were still wrapped around him, keeping him inside her.

Mika placed a gentle kiss against her brow before wrapping his hands around her bottom. He moved toward her bedroom. He bent at the waist and placed her softly on the bed.

Sarah felt desire unfurl inside her. She was just about to repeat something she would regret later.

~ * ~

The sun shone brightly through the opened curtain. Sarah groaned and rolled over. Her hand plopped against the soft linen. She was alone. Where did he run off to?

She sat up and looked around. Well, he wasn't in the room. *Did he leave?* Sarah stood and wrapped her robe around her. Last night was wild and wonderful, but today was a new day. Mika couldn't use it as leverage. She wouldn't let him.

Working her way through the house, she didn't spot him anywhere.

Where can he be? She heard a faint sound from the bathroom. There was no water running. Maybe he was using the toilet.

A splash caught her attention. What was he doing, playing in the sink or something? She knocked on the door. "Mika?"

She heard another splash before he answered.

"Yes?"

"What are you doing?"

"Um, taking a bath." His voice sounded muffled, like he had just woken up.

"What?" Maybe she needed a strong cup of coffee. "How long have you been in there?"

"Not long."

Did she hear his teeth chattering? "Okay. Well. You coming out any time soon?"

"Sure. Just give me a minute."

She heard more splashing before she heard a large bam. "You okay?"

"I'm fine. I'm fine. Just drying off now."

"See you in the kitchen then."

"You bet."

She shook her head and went to put coffee on. Whatever was going on with him was something she didn't really want to know. She watched the bathroom as she got coffee cups, cream, and sugar. He should have come out of the bathroom minutes ago. What could he be doing?

The coffee was ready by the time she saw him. He smiled as he sat down at the table. He took the pot out of her hands and poured both of them a drink. "This stuff is the best I've ever tasted."

"Don't have coffee where you come from?"

"Nope." He took a long drink, draining his cup in one gulp. After downing another cup, he spoke. "Really makes me feel awake too."

"That's the caffeine." She took a sip from her coffee. "Some people can't handle it. As fast as you're knocking those back, I have a feeling you're going to be flying. Why don't we go out for a while? Help you burn off some of that caffeine?"

"Okay." He swallowed another cup full before standing. "Whoa."

"Watch it, big boy." She offered a hand to steady him. "If you're not careful you just might crush me."

* * * *

Mika was like a big child. When they stopped at the park, he had to try out every ride. The swings were his favorite, but when he tried to flip the thing all the way around while swinging, they were kicked out of the park. His crestfallen face was priceless.

She fed him hamburgers this time, and he ate three. He ate like a whale, like he had never eaten any of that before. What was he going to do at the dinner tonight? She jumped in the shower first, not wanting to take a chance on him getting in there and never coming out. She now stood in her bedroom, putting the final touches on her makeup.

They just had to make it through the next few hours.

She heard that weird thump coming from the bathroom again. "I'm actually getting used to that." She pulled the dress she planned to wear out of her closet and placed it on her bed.

The bathroom door finally opened by the time she had her dress on. It was a simple black dress that clung to all the right places. It might be a bit dressy, but it made her feel good, and that was what counted.

Mika banged around the living room as she donned her jewelry. She hoped he'd be dressed by the time she finished. She was too nervous to stay in her room and wait. After checking her appearance one last time in the mirror, she slipped on her pumps and walked out of her room. "Mika, you decent?"

"Sort of."

What the heck did he mean by that? "Excuse me?"

"I'm having a problem."

Sarah straightened her shoulders and stepped into the room. She found him fighting with his crotch. It didn't take much to see what went wrong. Somehow he got the tail of his shirt caught in his zipper, and he was getting so frustrated he was making it worse.

"Stop." She came up to him and slapped his hands away. "How did you get it this bad? You haven't been out here that long."

"I don't know what happened." He stared down at her hands pulling at the zipper.

Sarah felt the heat of his gaze. She gave the zipper a couple of sharp tugs before she freed the shirt and pulled his zipper up.

187

She checked to make sure his shirt was buttoned properly before helping him with his jacket. "Nervous?"

"No. Excited. You?"

"Scared to death," she said in a soft voice.

"Why?" He helped her on with her wrap.

"I have a lot on the line." She didn't want to go into just how much was at stake. Her job, her security, her happiness. Sarah let out a pent up breath. Thinking about it only made it worse. "Let's go."

~ * ~

The site of the dinner dance was a big posh hotel near the beach. Her heart pounded in her chest as they climbed the stairs to the main ballroom. Now she had to do her best. So did her date. Sarah looked up at Mika only to find him smiling back at her. He had no clue.

They walked into the ballroom, into a crowd of people. Mika faded from sight as some of her friends crowded around her.

"Who's the cutie?" asked one.

"And does he have a brother?" giggled another.

Sarah latched on to him and pulled him to her side. "Ladies, this is Mika, my date."

They all sighed his name together, "Hi, Mika."

"Ladies. What a wonderful way to be greeted." Mika smiled at each of them.

Sarah felt just a little bit jealous. She had gotten so used to having all his attention she didn't want to share him.

"So, Mika, how did you meet Sarah?"

"At the beach."

"Really." The woman looked him up and down. "I've never seen anything like you at the beach."

"Guess you haven't hit the beach on the right day." Mika's comment brought laughter from the ladies.

Sarah watched as some of the women batted their eyelashes at him. A couple of others were even brave enough to touch him. It made her want to snatch them all baldheaded.

Mika, bless him, never left her side. Any of her previous dates would have completely forgotten her and gone for any of the women there.

She was grateful when the president of the company announced that dinner was served. They took their seats at their assigned table. To Sarah's chagrin, she found her boss to her right and the ditzy little blonde who delivered their mail on Mika's left.

As the blonde went on about her marvelous manicure, Sarah did everything she could not to make eye contact with anyone else at the table. She was afraid she'd say something she shouldn't. Not doing anything stupid was going to be hard enough. Sarah didn't want to complicate matters by speaking out of turn.

She popped an olive in her mouth and came close to choking on it when she heard the ditzy blonde ask Mika a very simple question. Actually, it was Mika's answer that caused the problem.

"Mika, you have a very unique accent. Where are you from?"

"Bottom of the ocean." He winked at Sarah before picking up his drink.

"Really? Do you know Flipper?"

"No, but I've heard of him." He took a quick sip amongst the chuckles heard around the table. "So, all of you work with Sarah?"

"Everyone at this table does, but we have a lot of different departments," said Mr. Milici "That's who the people at the other tables are."

Mika nodded.

Sarah played with her napkin. So far, Mika was holding his own. Maybe if everyone focused on him, they'd forget about her and her klutziness, and she'd make it through the night.

"This is a lovely hotel," said Mika. He watched as others started to eat their salad.

"Pride of the beach," said Mr. Milici. He picked up his fork the moment the server set the salad in front of him. Mika imitated him.

"I see why." Mika stabbed his fork into the salad and managed to get almost all of in on the fork in one shot.

Sarah felt color leave her face as he lifted the fork to his lips. *Please, don't shove the whole thing in your mouth.* But he did.

Mika munched away with a smile on his face until he found everyone staring at him. "It's very good," he mumbled through lettuce.

Barbara Donlon Bradley

Sarah wanted to crawl under the table. Making it through the night without an incident just flew out the window. She leaned over to speak to him softly. "You're supposed to eat a little bit at a time."

"Oh."

Was that all he had to say? Sarah stabbed at her salad and chewed on the few pieces she was able to spear. Bringing him was a mistake. She knew he had some crazy idiosyncrasies but thought he would behave better than this.

Now she had to dump him before he caused more trouble. But how?

Chapter Six

So how was she going to get him to leave before anything else happened? Subtle might not work, but she didn't want to make a scene either. Mika seemed clueless as he pushed the salad from his fork to his plate and started to eat like a normal person. Servers started to remove salad plates and replace them with the main course. Shrimp scampi. Okay this should be safe. Mika doesn't have to shell anything.

"What have they done to the shrimp?"

"Never had shrimp scampi before, son?" asked her boss.

Mika looked at Sarah and saw fear in her eyes. "Can't say I have." He looked around at different people at the table. "Most of the time my family eats shrimp plain. We've always liked it that way."

"You'll love this. The spices really enhance the taste," said Mr. Milici. He rubbed his hands together when the server sat his plate in front of him.

Mika imitated him and picked up his fork. Sarah made sure she had Mika's attention then she showed him how to eat the shrimp without embarrassing her. She hoped he got the silent message.

Their meal passed without any more trouble. After the plates were cleared off, the president of the company stood up on the stage once more to hand out awards and bonuses. Once that was done, the music began. Mika tugged at his collar.

"You okay?" asked Sarah. He looked a little green.

"Just a little hot." He picked up a glass of water and downed it in one gulp. He then picked up every water goblet on the table and downed the contents in seconds. Once he finished with the ones on their table, he started grabbing ones from the other tables.

"You can't just take the water like that. Let me get one of the servers." Sarah looked around to see if she could find one.

"Can't wait that long." He stood up, spied the fountain outside the huge bay windows, and headed for the doors.

Sarah sat for a moment before his words penetrated her thoughts. Oh no. She jumped up and followed him as fast as she could. All she needed was for him to do something stupid.

~ * ~

Mika knew he needed to feel water against his skin before he suffocated. His time away from the water had been too long. Sleeping in the tub had saturated his cells somewhat but not enough to last him all evening. Besides, fresh water wouldn't saturate his body properly at this stage. He needed saltwater. It was the only thing that would heal him.

Using his nose, he sniffed for the life-giving water he needed. The huge fountain he spotted from the ballroom didn't have what he needed. He caught a faint whiff to his right and turned that way. Around the corner from the big fountain, he found a small fish pond. Thank goodness, humans captured the darnedest things. They had several saltwater fish in the pond. Perfect for his needs.

He took off his shoes and socks and inhaled deeply again. There was a small alcove at the edge of the pond where people could sit and watch the fish. Mika smiled as he stepped into the darkened shade. His shoes and socks went under the bench along with his pants, shirt, tie, and jacket. The cool brisk breeze stirred the hairs on his chest and arms.

Naked, he slipped into the pond.

~ * ~

Sarah came around the corner just in time to see Mika slip into the small saltwater pond. As she stalked toward the pond, she smacked her forehead in frustration. Was he completely mad or just partially? "Mika!" she bit out.

No answer. She didn't want to scream his name and attract any unwanted attention, but she had to get him out of the pond as quickly as possible. "Mika!"

He popped his head up over the edge of the pond. His eyes rounded at the sight of her. "What are you doing here?"

"Trying to stop you." She came to the edge where he rested. "If anyone saw you…"

"We'd both have a lot to explain. Please, go into the alcove so no one will see you." He dipped back down below the lip and disappeared from sight.

"What are you doing?" she said. "You have to come out now."

"I can't. I need about ten minutes, and I'll be fine."

A splash flew up in the air and rained down on the walk close to Sarah, making her jump back into the alcove. "We don't have a few minutes."

A couple passed nearby, making her duck deeper into the alcove and remain silent. The moment they were out of earshot, she started right back up. "You have to come out now."

"Sarah." His voice was deep and seductive. "There is something you should know."

She couldn't see him below the lip of the pond. "We don't have time for this."

"Then we need to make time." He came up to the alcove where she could see him.

There was something wrong about the way he floated in the water. She couldn't see his legs, but the pond couldn't be more than two or three feet deep. He should be sitting on the bottom. Naked. "Where are your legs?"

"I need you to listen to me." He floated closer. "There's something about me you need to know." He sounded so serious.

"Fine. We'll talk, but once you're out of the water and fully clothed."

"Hey, Sarah." She jerked her head in the direction of the voice. It was the dippy blonde from their table. "Hi, Phoebe."

"Where's your handsome man?" She looked about.

"He'll be along in a minute." Sarah wondered why Phoebe didn't notice Mika in the pond.

Phoebe looked disappointed. "Okay. Um, the dancing has started. And I've been sent out to collect you."

"I'll be right there." Sarah knew Mr. Milici had sent Phoebe. The veiled threat had been hard to miss. She was expected to be inside and socializing. "Mika, please come out of there."

"I can't."

"You have to," she begged.

"Sarah, look at me."

"What?" She pushed her hair out of her face and stared down at the biggest fin she had ever seen. Blood rushed from her face when she realized it was attached to Mika. "What the hell?"

She stumbled backward, trying to get away from the nightmare she saw in front of her. *He can't be half fish. What is he? A mermaid?* This was too much to comprehend. Sarah staggered back into the ballroom and hoped she could function long enough to make her boss happy.

People spoke to her, but she didn't know what they said, her mind was still wrapped around what she saw. It had to be the trick of the light because mermaids didn't exist. They were myth, legend, figments of the imagination.

Yet, she had seen it, or him. Her mind tried to dismiss it. Until Mika walked back into the ballroom and straight to her.

"I can't talk to you." She tried to sidestep him.

"Sarah." He touched her arm gently, like he didn't want to frighten her.

"Nope. Not now." She was able to scoot around him and headed straight to Mr. Milici. Why she expected her boss to protect her was beyond her, but she followed her instincts.

Mika was right behind her. She could feel him. Sarah was so focused on avoiding Mika she didn't see the president of the company in front of her. Bam!

"Oh no." She hit him so hard she was sure she heard the clonking of their heads. Her chest hurt from crushing the glass the president had been holding. Now they both wore a deep red burgundy all over the front of their outfits. Sarah fared better since she wore black. The president didn't. His white shirt now showed pink.

"I'm so sorry!" Sarah backed up and tripped over Mika's feet. "I'm sorry."

"It's okay, things like this happen."

Sarah nodded, but she couldn't forgive herself. She had been doing so well. She hadn't stuck a sleeve in her meal. Dropped a drink or silverware. Tripped over anything. Until now. Mr. Milici headed toward them. She knew what was going to happen next. She got to her feet as quickly as she could. If her boss was going to fire her here in front of everyone, she was going to be face to face with him.

"Sir, I'm so sorry."

He turned to Sarah. "You, young lady, knew what the consequences were if something like this happened."

Words failed her, so she nodded for the second time. She brushed by Mika and headed to the doors. Nothing mattered anymore.

~ * ~

Sarah raced away from him, blindly heading out the main doors. He dashed after her, hoping to calm her down enough to explain things better. She had paused to get her car, but when she turned and found him following her, she took off running again. His quickness stopped her.

"I need some time to myself. To think." Fear etched her eyes. He knew she couldn't wrap her mind around his true nature. As much as his father tried to warn him about how humans reacted to their reality, it hurt to see her afraid of him.

Mika spotted the car flying up the road just seconds before it hit Sarah. She flew in the air and landed with an awful thud. He was at her side in seconds.

The driver bolted out his car. "Oh God, is she okay?" The driver whipped out a small phone and placed a call. He talked into it for a moment and then snapped it shut. "The police and an ambulance are on the way."

People poured out of the hotel to gawk at the accident. A loud scream filled the air as cars with flashing lights came closer. They screeched to a halt, and more people surrounded him. Someone pulled him to his feet and moved him out of the way while they worked on her.

Focusing, he listened to the conversations. The men who came out of the cars with the flashing lights wanted to know what had happened while they spoke to the driver. The woman who came out of the big box on wheels shouted orders to the man who rode with her, asking for different items inside the box. They became more frantic in their work.

Mika watched as they strapped Sarah down in a small portable bed. He saw people pointing at him. The woman came to his side.

"She's your date? What's her name?"

"Sarah. What is wrong?" He could see worry in her eyes.

"We're going to get her to the hospital. The doctors there are excellent. They'll do everything they can for her."

"But you don't think she's going to make it."

She patted him on the arm. "Can someone take you to the hospital?"

He needed to talk to his dad. "I'll find a way there."

Mika watched as the vehicles pulled away. He ran to the ocean edge only a block from the hotel. He dove into the shore breakers, feeling the change overtake him. The clothing he wore tore off his body as his tail formed.

He streaked through the water, pushing faster and faster. He ploughed into his father. "I need your help."

"What's wrong?" He gripped Mika's shoulders and held him at arm's length.

"Sarah. A car hit her. The humans don't think she's going to live."

"And what do you want me to do, son?"

"I don't know." Mika's shoulders slumped. "Make her one of us?"

"I can't do that without her permission."

"I can't live without her." He straightened his shoulders. "I won't live without her. If you won't help me, I know who will."

"You'll not go to the sea witch."

"Then you'll help me?" Mika couldn't keep the hope out of his voice.

"Yes."

~ * ~

The brightly lit hospital smelled of death and hope. Mika didn't know what to think of the building.

"This is where humans take their sick. This is also where their children are born." His father led the way into the hospital.

No wonder the building had such conflicting odors. They stepped up to a sweet gray-haired woman sitting behind a glassed-in desk.

"We're looking for Sarah?" Mika's father turned to look at him.

"Her last name, son? We need her last name."

"Oh, McIntire. Sarah McIntire. She was in a car accident."

The woman punched keys on a board in front of her. "She's in intensive care. Are you related?"

"Not yet," responded Mika's father.

"Oh, engaged? How sweet. I think they'll let you in, sir, but not your father. Go to the elevators, and go up to the third floor. Then follow the red stripe on the floor. It will take you to the unit. Once you're there you'll find the nursing station."

"What have the doctors said?"

"You'll have to ask them, sir. They don't give me any information."

They did as the woman said. Mika picked up speed as they walked along.

His father grabbed his arm. "What's wrong?"

"I can feel her. She's weak and in pain."

"Then we need to hurry."

~ * ~

After he and his father made sure no one was working on her, they hid themselves from view and walked into her room. Mika sat on the edge of the bed, holding Sarah's hand. "She doesn't look good."

"What caused this?" His father frowned at him.

"She saw me and my tail." Mika dropped his gaze with his words.

"Mika."

"I know, I know, no one is supposed to see us change. Just help her, Dad."

"I need to talk to her alone."

Mika nodded and stepped out of the room.

~ * ~

She felt someone rubbing the inside of her wrist. "How are you feeling, Sarah?"

She opened one eye and found a kind looking man sitting on her bed. Her throat hurt too much to speak, but she was able to squeeze his hand.

"My name is Dion. I'm Mika's father. I need to ask you a few questions. Can you speak?"

197

Barbara Donlon Bradley

"It hurts," she squeaked.

"I can fix that." He placed a small shell on her throat. "Better?"

"Much." Sarah touched her throat. "How did you do that?"

"A little bit of magic." He smiled.

"Mermaid magic?" She frowned.

"So he's told you about us, huh? He wasn't supposed to."

"It wasn't his fault." Sarah touched his arm. "I sort of caught him in the act."

"How do you feel about that?" He brushed hair out of her eyes.

"I have no idea." She broke eye contact with him. "I barely know Mika."

"Then why did you let him into your life."

"I needed a date." Sarah picked at the sheet covering her. "Okay, so maybe there was another reason. But he's hit me blindside."

"True. Mika is well known for that." He smiled.

"Really?" She looked at Dion. "I hadn't noticed."

"Now you're just being sarcastic." Dion sat quietly for a few moments. "If you only wanted a date, why were you intimate with my son?"

"What makes you say that?" Sarah blushed.

"You glow. There's this thing that happens when a human mates with mer-folks. Think of it as a residue. One only other mermaids can see."

"Mermaids. Is that what you call yourselves?"

"No." Dion laughed. "But it's the name most humans know us by. I thought it would be easier. You're very good at avoiding a conversation you don't want to have, aren't you?"

She nodded. "Can't help it. This hasn't been one of my better days."

"That's one of the reasons I wanted to talk to you. I can offer you a new choice."

"I don't know." She sighed and slumped her shoulders.

"Will you hear me out?"

"I guess."

"Your human body has been heavily damaged. I think beyond your medicine, but not beyond ours. I can heal you." He tightened his hold a little. "If I do, you can't come back on land."

"Why not?" She didn't like the way this conversation was going.

"What have they told you so far?"

"Nothing. I guess I haven't woken up until now."

"You are in a coma. One they are afraid you won't come out of. These humans are saying you have brain damage. Something they can't fix."

"They think I'm going to be a vegetable the rest of my life?"

He nodded. As if on cue, two medical staff members came in to check on her. They didn't notice the man at her side nor did they see her alert. "This is such a sad story, doctor. I understand her fiancé is outside."

Sarah watched a woman write down her vitals then leave the room. The doctor stood there a little longer before he too left the room.

"Why didn't they see you?"

"I can use glamour to blind people to my appearance. Most of us can. One of the reasons why mermaids have never been noticed. We can also pick up thoughts. It's not quite the same as reading the mind, but it helps us fit in with your world quickly. We can also grant wishes."

"You mean I can ask to have the last few hours back, and you could give them to me?" Her voice was hopeful.

"Yes. If that is what you want." Dion stroked her hand. "Or I can make you a mermaid."

"I can't breathe underwater." *Is he crazy? I can't become a mermaid.*

"You can, with my help. Many humans have joined us under the water and started new lives."

"But I can't come home again." She looked away at the row of equipment they had next to her bed. Sarah didn't know what to do. There was nothing to hold her in her present life, but she wasn't sure she could give it up. "Am I wired to all of this?"

He nodded. "I don't have much time."

"I don't know what to do." She covered her eyes with her hands. "I'm by far the kluziest thing on the planet. If there is a hole in the ground, I will find it and most likely fall in it or trip over it. My boss makes me so nervous, it's worse at work. When Mika came into my life, he was the one who was stumbling around."

"Not being used to land can do that to you."

She laughed and moved her hands from her face. "I bet. Would water do that to me?"

"Actually you'd have a lot more grace. There's something about water that makes everyone in the realm more fluid, no pun intended."

"That's a good selling point." She sat up a little with help from Dion. "Mika's very sweet. Everything was so new to him I was able to see my world in a whole new way. It took all the grime away for a while. But after the way this evening went it all came crashing down around me. I have a job I hate, work for a man who sure doesn't like me, and live in a world that has so much sadness I get overwhelmed at times."

"Then I have some work to do. We must make it look like you died, Sarah. It will explain your disappearance."

~ * ~

Sarah stood at the edge of the water holding Mika's hand. Fear, strong and quick, raced through her. "I'm not sure about this."

"I've been told it doesn't hurt much." Mika squeezed her hand.

"Oh, great. Sounds like a root canal." She took a deep breath. "Okay. Let's get this over with before I change my mind."

Mika smiled and slipped a shell necklace around her neck. "You need to get in the water now."

She picked up the necklace hanging around her neck. "What is this, a joke?"

"No." Mika looked at the tide. "Oh good, since you won't step into the water, there's a wave coming in to help us out."

"What are you—oof." Sarah felt her feet come out from under her. When she looked down her legs looked funny, like they were glued together.

"That joke is starting to work. Go out in the water a little farther."

Sarah walked out a little deeper and felt a weird tingling sensation. "What's happening?"

Mika looked around before stripping off his clothes. He walked to the edge of the surf and sat down. As the waves came in, he moved out to her side. His blue fin appeared the moment water covered it. "Your change the first few times will take longer."

"So I can go back on land?" She watched her legs shimmer, allowing scales to show.

"From time to time."

"Cool."

"You ready to see your new world?"

Sarah flipped her large blue fin in the water and smiled. "I can't wait."

About the Author

Writing for Barbara Donlon Bradley started innocently enough, like most she kept diaries, journals, and wrote an occasional letter but she also had a vivid imagination and wrote scenes and short stories adding characters to her favorite shows and comic books. As time went on she found the passion for writing to be a strong drive for her. Humor is also very strong in her life. No matter how hard she tries to write something deep and dark, it will never happen. That humor bleeds into her writing. Since she can't beat it she has learned to use it to her advantage. Now she lives in Tidewater Virginia with two cats, one mother in law – she's 85 now, her husband and teenage son.

bdbradley3@cox.net
www.barbaradonlonbradley.com

For more works by Ms. Bradley, go to
www.melange-books.com

www.ingramcontent.com/pod-product-compliance
Lightning Source LLC
Chambersburg PA
CBHW031421250626
47155CB00004B/1581